# PAPA
# HAMLET

# ARNO HOLZ & JOHANNES SCHLAF

# PAPA HAMLET

*Translated from the German and
with an afterword by James J. Conway*

**RIXDORF EDITIONS BERLIN 2021**

'Papa Hamlet', 'A Death' and 'Translator's Introduction' by Arno Holz and Johannes Schlaf were first published in German as 'Papa Hamlet', 'Ein Tod' and 'Einleitung des Übersetzers', respectively, in *Papa Hamlet*, issued by Carl Reissner in Leipzig, 1889, initially credited to 'Bjarne P. Holmsen' in the 'translation of Dr Bruno Franzius', who was also originally credited with the introduction. The new Foreword to *Papa Hamlet* by Arno Holz and Johannes Schlaf was first published in German in the anthology *Neue Gleise. Gemeinsames von Arno Holz und Johannes Schlaf*, by F. Fontane, Berlin, 1892.

'The Paper Passion' by Arno Holz and Johannes Schlaf first appeared in German as 'Die papierne Passion' in *Freie Bühne für modernes Leben* (2 April 1890).

'A Garrett Idyll' by Johannes Schlaf first appeared in German as 'Ein Dachstubenidyll' in *Die Gesellschaft* (May 1890).

This translation, anthology and afterword © 2021 James J. Conway

*Papa Hamlet*
first published Rixdorf Editions, Berlin, 2021

Design by Svenja Prigge; front cover adapted from an image by Fritz Schoen

Printed by Totem.com.pl, Inowrocław, Poland

ISBN: 978-3-947325-11-5

RixdorfEditions.com

# CONTENTS

PAPA HAMLET

# PAPA HAMLET

I

What? Was that Niels Thienwiebel? Niels Thienwiebel, the great, unsurpassed Hamlet from Trondheim? I eat the air, and am promise-crammed? You cannot better feed capons so? …

'Hey! Horatio!'

'Just a moment! Just a moment, Nielsie! Where's the fire? Should I bring the playing cards?'

'N … no! I mean …'

– – 'Damn it to hell! That, that's a, a – bathtub!'

Poor little Ole Nissen was almost about to trip over it. He had just come from the kitchen and was now on all fours looking for his blue pince-nez, which had fallen off his nose again in the rush.

'Huh? What? What did you say?!'

'What is it, Nielsie? What?'

'Numbskull!'

'But Thiiienwiebel!'

'Amalie?! I …'

'Ach! Well would you look at that! So that's it!'

'Huh?! What?! Great rogue! My rogue! My rogue. Amalie! Heh! What?'

Amalie smiled. A little drawn.

'A capital fellow!'

'A little demon! My little demon! My little demon! Heh! What, Amalie? My little demon!'

Amalie nodded. A little tired.

'Yes, Herr Thienwiebel! Yes indeed!'

But Frau Wachtel struggled in vain. Herr Thienwiebel, the great, unsurpassed Hamlet from Trondheim, did not wish to let go of his little demon.

'Huh, old boy? Huh?'

'Indeed, Nielsie! Indeed, a … a … magnificent specimen! A magnificent specimen!'

'Hoo, hoo, hoo, hop!! Hoo, hoo, hoo, hop!! Boom!!!'

The great Thienwiebel was wallowing in delight. He was even standing on one leg now. The wadding was flapping from the back of his checked dressing gown.

'But Thiiienwiebel!'


II


'To be or not to be, that is the question:

Whether 'tis nobler in the mind, the slings and arrows

of outrageous fortune, or …

or? … Atrocious!'

The great Thienwiebel paused again.

'This, this is intolerable! This is intolerable!!'

The five small yellow rags behind the stove, which were hung up there to dry on a washing line, had completely thrown his concentration again.

'Disgusting!'

Now he was standing bitterly at the window with his hands in his dressing gown pockets.

The sky was deep blue above the roofs; the sparrows were already squabbling in the wet gutters from which the last of the snow was dripping; it was wonderful weather for going out.

'Poor Yorick!'

A shade more gloomy yet, the great Thienwiebel had thrown himself backwards over the small, low sofa covered in blue calico and was now staring mournfully over the tips of his green, well-worn slippers at Amalie.

Her thin, clay-coloured hair had not yet been fixed, her nightshirt seemed even dirtier than usual today and of course it was open again in the front; crouched on her footstool, she was carelessly using a rubber tube to feed the cherry-red little customer, who suddenly looked as ugly as a little frog.

'Poor Yorick!'

Herr Thienwiebel had risen again with a sigh and now resumed his prior pacing.

'… or? or …
To take arms against a sea of troubles,
And by opposing end them. – To die – to sleep –

No more! –'

Once at the window he couldn't deny himself another short break.

The sun was just setting outside. The roofs looked ginger red. But one look down at his old, worn dressing gown made him pull himself together again and resume his monologue from the start.

'To be or not to be, that is the question:
Whether 'tis nobler in mind …

Ach, rubbish!!'

With a start the Shakespeare, which he had just now torn from his dressing gown pocket, was flung onto the table, where it found itself in the company of an ethanol cooker, an earthen brown milk pot without a handle, an old, sooty towel, a glass lamp and a photograph of the great Thienwiebel in a mora wood frame.

'Hey! Horatio! Horatio!! … No one home! No one home …'

Quite ruined, he had hurled himself back on the sofa and was now absorbed by the tragic tableau of a child's dirty pinafore which lay on the floor before him next to a broken box of Swedish matches.

'Curse it! If we could at least go out, Amalie! But I fear … I fear … the world is not enlightened enough to let a Niels Thienwiebel in dressing gown and top hat go his way unmolested!'

But Amalie didn't even answer. The little lobster-red thing absorbed her full attention. His sucking had now contracted the whole hose.

'Yes! That's how it is! That's how it is, Amalie! But they still haven't written to me! They have people there, people – people? Pah! Bunglers! O spurns that patient merit of the unworthy takes!'

Now Amalie, who was already familiar this refrain, looked up.

'Yes … in the end it might be good if you …'

Her voice sounded hoarse, husky.

'Yes, it will happen! Perhaps … with my weakness and melancholy …'

The little lobster was smacking his lips! His bottle was all but empty now.

'I shall have to go there myself and accept whatever they dare offer me! Life is brutal, Amalie! Curse it! If only one had a coat to go out in!'

His tone was quite mad now, he had stretched himself over the sofa again.

A long pause …

The roofs outside had gradually turned brown.

The sun on the big round chimney across the way had faded.

Over in her corner, Frau Thienwiebel now began to cough.

'Good God, Niels! I have to inhale! Here, take the child!'

'Naturally! Nanny now, too! O God, your only jig-maker! What should a man do but be merry? Quiet, lobster!!'

The little lobster was silent again. He had never been so stunned.

'There! Take it! Chew it! Eat! Swallow it!'

The great Thienwiebel had now even managed to stuff the rubber teat into the mouth of his wayward offspring. One could not ask more of him than that!

In the meantime Amalie had opened the stove-pipe and taken out a small, green-glazed saucepan. From it arose a vapour with an odour of sage. Once she had put the little dish on a chair next to the stove and herself on the footstool before it, she opened her mouth and slowly inhaled the hot concoction.

The great Thienwiebel, who in the meantime had positioned himself on the edge of the table with his impertinent little lobster-red creature, watched her thoughtfully.

'Hmmm! Do you know what, Amalie?'

'Hmmm??'

'Do you know what? Our method of feeding the child is completely wrong, Amalie!'

'What!'

'The method, I say! A *wrong-headed* method Amalie!'

'But …'

'Take my word for it! It is unnatural, Amalie!'

'Yes, dear God …'

'It's unnatural … we should not make the child drink from the bottle!'

'No? Well, from what then?'

'You should just feed him yourself!'

'Me?'

'Certainly, Amalie!'

'Oh, dear God! Me! Myself!'

'Well! Why not?'

'Me?? Now, with my weak, sick chest?'

'Nonsense! That's in your mind, Amalie! I tell you, you are completely healthy. You are completely healthy, I say! … What's more, a child can only truly thrive if the mother nurses it herself.'

Herr Thienwiebel had now become most fervent. He seemed to have completely forgotten his boredom from earlier. He didn't even seem to have noticed that the little wriggling grub on his knees had dropped the rubber teat again.

'Take my word for it, Amalie! I tell you, the most natural method is always the best! Think about it: what else are the Negresses to do! They have no bottles! They simply feed their children themselves, you see … and, and – well! And they thrive on it! Thrive! Well?'

'Yes, Niels, but I'm not a Negress!'

The great Thienwiebel gave her a superior smile.

'Well, don't … heehee! Don't misunderstand me, Amalie! Heehee!'

Amalie had bent low over her sage pot again.

'I merely wished to indicate to you through a … a … well! through an example, let's say, that the most natural way is always the most prudent. I just don't see why Negresses should have anything over us!'

'But they are healthy!'

'Come now! This illness, it's all in your mind, Amalie!'

'My mind?'

'Certainly, Amalie! I maintain …'

Amalie had now grown a little impatient.

'Nonsense! It's better to not let the child scream like that!'

'And *that* is another of your preconceptions, Amalie! What harm does it do! I have read that there is nothing healthier! It dilates the lungs! But – er ... as I said! You should feed the child yourself! Certainly today's culture, the culture of the European sphere ...'

The culture passed Amalie by. She abided only by the admonitions she had come to hear so often of late.

'Oh yes! Oh yes! Yes indeed! Certainly! With our way of life! Living on coffee and buttered bread all day long! I should like to know how the poor grub is meant to thrive!'

'Ha! To live in the rank sweat of an enseamed bed, stew'd in corruption, and making love over the nasty sty! Is that it? You mean to say that I am to blame for our situation, Amalie!'

'Well! Am I?'

'Woman!!?'

'Morning!'

The door, at which someone had been knocking in vain for some time, was thrown wide open at that moment, and there, prancing in his ever-present havelock which had probably once been field grey, a huge black slouch hat pressed low over his small, cheerful, pale face, was little Ole Nissen.

'Morning! Don't let me disturb you, friends! I beg you! No fuss, Nielsie! No fuss! I know! Trying a new scene! So, as I was saying ... damn it! That's a hard beast!'

He had just flopped down in the middle of the little calico sofa and almost lost his Egyptian cigarette, which was crookedly clamped between his teeth.

'So, as I was saying! I'm walking down the embankment feeling utterly miserable. Huh? And who should I see there? The sewer inspector! Well, who else? The sewer inspector, of course! Fancy marriage, villa in Bratsberg, ha! and so on and so forth. You can imagine! So, of course, he drags me to Hiddersen's at once and interrogates me … Well, old chap? How are you? … So naturally I say: rotten! Rotten! … hmmm! You know what? You could actually do a portrait of my lady wife! … hmmm! With pleasure, my friend! With pleasure! But – erm … paints, you see – ah, canvas, frame and so on … huh! What? Great turkey!'

Ole Nissen was now jingling the fine, fancy crowns in his pockets.

'Frau Wachtel! Frau Wachtell!! Frau Wachtelll!!!'

The house of Thienwiebel was bathing in delight once more. Its quarrels were deferred for a time once again.

'Huh! And this? Is it butter? And this? Huh? Is it ham? Huh? And this? Huh? Bring the good silver! Silence!!'

Little Ole was over the moon again today …

Once the 'good silver' had finally been cleared away and two-thirds of the punch bowl emptied, Frau Wachtel had even 'scared up' the playing cards. It was simply wonderful! The great Thienwiebel had his Turkish fez on, Ole Nissen even gallantly offered his Egyptian cigarettes to old Madame Wachtel, who, however, fled from them indignantly back to her kitchen; Amalie valiantly smoked with the men. She was transported back to her old Ophelia years. 'Oh, Thienwiebel! Niels!! Beloved!!!'

The great Thienwiebel stood there and wept.

'Am I a coward? – Ha! Plucks off my beard, and blows it in my face! No, fair Ophelia! No! Do not weep! My fate cries out, and makes each petty artery in this body as hardy as the Nemean lion's nerve! … what, old Jephthah? … Nay, do not think I flatter! For what advancement may I hope from thee that no revenue hast but thy good spirits, to feed and clothe thee?'

His voice broke off, the hand that he had placed on his shoulder trembled. –

Finally, when the old glass lamp was burning no more than a wan light and the magnificent Egyptian cigarettes had laid a fine silvery grey, finger-thick ring of fog around its green dome, little Ole Nissen was moved as well.

Little by little he had moved across to the fair Ophelia on the little blue calico-covered sofa and from that point would only address her as 'Kitty'. Now he had finally got hold of her hands and covered them with his kisses.

The great Thienwiebel raised no objection. He had spread his hands over them in blessing and could only stammer out his heart.

'This presence knows, and you must needs have heard, how I am punish'd with sore distraction!'

Meanwhile, back in its corner, the little lobster had been left to its distress. He had already cried himself to sleep several times. But now he had woken up again and could not for the life of him find his rubber teat. The fair Ophelia did not hear him. She had long since fallen asleep in her corner of the sofa. He was screaming like a stuck pig now.

The great Thienwiebel naturally had no time for the rogue, particularly now. He had grabbed little Ole Nissen, who could hardly keep his small, watery blue eyes open now, by the front of his coat collar and merely declaimed again:

'Tis a chough, Horatio! A chough! But, as I say, spacious in the possession of dirt!'

## III

For it could not be! But he was pigeon-liver'd, the great Thienwiebel, and lacked gall …

He had of late – wherefore he knew not? – lost all his mirth, forgone all custom of exercises; and indeed it went so heavily with his disposition that this goodly frame, the earth, seemed to him a sterile promontory. This most excellent canopy, the air, look you, this brave o'erhanging firmament, this majestical roof fretted with golden fire, why, it appeared no other thing to him than a foul and pestilent congregation of vapours. What a piece of work was a man! How noble in reason! How infinite in faculty! In form and moving how express and admirable! in action how like an angel! in apprehension how like a god! the beauty of the world! The paragon of animals! And yet, to him, what was this quintessence of dust? Man delighted not him: no, nor woman neither. The time was out of joint! Was it to be believed? But – er

– still they hadn't written to him. They were ungrateful in Christiania. Poor Yorick!

To die, to sleep … perchance to dream? …

In the meantime, however, it certainly seemed that certain respects were going to make so long life of poor Yorick's calamity. In any case, at least those impudent life drawing students down in the academy had the opportunity to capture the great, unsurpassed Hamlet from Trondheim as a dying warrior in the fine, long morning hours for a full fortnight. Naturally this was a humiliation, but it brought money in. Unfortunately, it wasn't enough.

Now whenever 'poor Yorick' came home at midday with the appetite of a man who had been chopping oak logs for twenty-four hours without pause and fell upon the large bowl, covered as a precaution, that the fair Ophelia had placed on the table directly opposite the photograph, it usually contained nothing more than a vaguely green, thin potato soup with at best a few small, jet-black pieces of bacon floating here and there. Poor Yorick! …

Amalie appeared not to have put her nightshirt in the washing tub since time immemorial. Why get dressed up? They were at home, after all.

'Isn't that right, Thienwiebel?'

The great Thienwiebel considered it beneath his dignity to answer. He had just thrown himself back into his old, comfortable dressing gown from which admittedly the wadding was no longer hanging, but only because so little of it remained.

With his William open, he had thrown himself

right on his back over the little blue calico sofa.

> 'O, that this too too solid flesh would melt
> Thaw and resolve itself into a dew!
> Or that the Everlasting had not fix'd
> His canon 'gainst self-slaughter! O God! O God!
> How weary, stale, flat and unprofitable,
> seem to me all the uses of this world!
> Fie on't! ah fie!'

Amalie, who had sat down again on her plump little footstool next to the stove and had just dipped her bread and dripping into her coffee, now looked up, a little puzzled. But when 'poor Yorick' stopped reading and, having closed his William, turned his head to the wall, quite contrary to his usual habit, she felt a little uneasy.

She pondered a short while; but then, finally, she had made up her mind. Her voice sounded even more pitiful than usual.

'I want to take in sewing, Niels.'

'No, Amalie! Never! Never! That I will never tolerate! That would be an unpardonable neglect of your most sacred maternal duties!'

He had jumped up again, indignant.

'No, Amalie! Never! Not … while memory holds a seat in this … distracted globe!'

He had struck his forehead melodramatically.

Amalie felt calm again and was now biting heartily into her bread and dripping …

'Come in?'

It was Frau Wachtel. She had brought more milk for the little one.

The great Thienwiebel could not but have him baptised with the name of Fortinbras.

'Well, little dumpling? Are you bored? Oh, my little mouse! Oh!'

For she found Amalie to be somewhat negligent in her most sacred maternal duties, and she often took the liberty of a little inspection.

For Frau Rosine Wachtel was in possession of a good heart. And that must have been true, because she said it herself, and shed tears each time she did so. However, this possession had never been much of a hazard to her. Because no one had yet run off, and she always got her money; even if that often took a fair bit of work. Frau Rosine Wachtel could assure everyone of that … 'Oh, you little grub! Oh, my little cherub! Have they stuck you in a basket!'

The good Frau Wachtel was most moved. But suddenly, for some reason, probably because there seemed to be someone coming up the stairs out in the corridor, she felt it better to quickly see to her kitchen again …

The great Thienwiebel, who had been waiting a little impatiently until her round, trivial back had finally disappeared behind the door, because he again felt something like a soliloquy stirring within, had now tragically approached the small, round mirror above the dresser from which his handsome, noble Apollonian head was now nodding mournfully.

'O, my old friend! Thy face is valenced since I saw thee last!'

Amalie no longer concerned herself with him. She knew her great husband.

'O, my old friend!'

Was that his hair? His beautiful, celebrated, blue-black hair? A cruel nature of things had kept him from having it curled for weeks now. It now fell in strands, thick and plump, into his forehead, that lofty arch of majestic thoughts, just like this dressy, narrow-dugged time.

'O, my old friend!'

Once he believed himself sufficiently prepared for the sublime mission he had in mind, he now gravely turned to look at the small, yellow basket that was placed across two chairs close to the bed.

'Poor little human! What evil star condemned you to this misery!'

The poor little human wriggled at him and laughed.

'But quiet! Quiet! I shall apply my all! I shall apply my full strength! I will work, friend! I will work! I will defy destiny; from it I will wring that one day you shall take the position in this harsh world that your talents merit … Yes! Thus conscience does make cowards of us all. And thus the native hue of resolution is sicklied o'er with the pale cast of thought, and enterprises of great pith and moment with this regard their currents turn awry, and lose the name of action!'

His voice quaked, his dressing gown tassels, which he had forgotten to tie, trembled behind him.

Amalie had now put her bread and dripping aside again.

'Niels, I would sooner take in sewing!'

'Never! Never! Do not speak of it, Amalia! By my wrath! Do not speak of it!'

Amalie was now calmer than ever.

Her nice bread and dripping was, thank God, not quite finished. The great Thienwiebel's concentration was somewhat thrown, and he had some difficulty recovering it. Having picked the Shakespeare up from the floor again, he now held it behind his back among the strands of wadding, his fingers clamped around its red leather cover and, pained, nodded down at the astonished little bundle. It had barely dared to mutter the whole time.

'I know ... I know I am dying, friend! I am dying! – The potent poison quite o'er-crows my spirit. I cannot live to hear the news from England; But I do prophesy the election lights on Fortinbras ... Thou livest; report me and my cause aright to the unsatisfied!'

Little Fortinbras had become quite grave now. He had never heard his big papa talk to him in such a human way.

'The unsatisfied ...'

Outside the rain, which since early morning had covered the brown roofs across the way as though with gloss varnish, splashed from the window sill, under which the fair Ophelia had of course again forgotten to hang the water tank; it had now gradually crept down the grey wallpaper and right under the little blue calico sofa. The two burned matchsticks were already floating languorously on the little pond underneath. Suddenly something unforeseen seemed to have stung the great Thienwiebel again.

'Amalie! Amalie!!'

'What is it now, Thienwiebel!'

She had not even turned around.

'Amalie! It cannot be denied: the child has quite extraordinary abilities! He just laughed at me. He's having a good old conversation with me!'

Amalie merely grunted peevishly.

'I bet we could teach him the rudiments of speech, Amalie!'

'Hmmm? All right! Say: *ah!* Well?! *a-a-ah* …'

The good little Fortinbras was so baffled he didn't know what to do. He had clawed his two fat little hands right and left into the rim of the basket and now, with his head laid back, he quite happily *ay*'d at his big Papa.

'Not *ay*, my boy! Say *ah!* You have to say *ah!* And? Well? *Aaaah!* …'

'Oh, leave it be! He can't do that yet!'

Amalie had finally thought it advisable to intervene.

'What?! He can't do it?! Do not say that, Amalie! Do not say that! For he's *my* boy! Huh? Are you my boy? Huh?'

'But he's barely three months old!'

'So? So? Well, hmmm … I don't wish to argue with you, Amalie! Only you must have noticed earlier that he understood entirely what I meant!'

Amalie yawned. She gave up. It was no use! It didn't matter! Either way!

But the great Thienwiebel was not yet satisfied. He couldn't cast aside his idea that easily.

'No, certainly, Amalie! The boy warrants the highest of hopes!'

'Oh …'

'Well! What is so unusual about that, Amalie? There are more things in heaven and earth, Amalie, than are dreamt of in your philosophy!'

Amalie merely yawned again.

'… And now, good friends,
As you are friends, scholars and soldiers,
Give me one poor request!'

They gave it to him.

It was really too good of the great Thienwiebel!

But he had now bent low over his sweet little Fortinbras, who warranted such high hopes, and he now wished to – oh, for the first time, for the first time, in a long, long time, Horatio! – to kiss him on his pale little forehead.

But it was not to come to that. He reeled back before he had even discharged his fine deed.

'Ha!'

His eyes rolled, his fists were clenched, the two red tassels on the back of his dressing-gown shook with indignation.

'Ha!'

Here was the resounding solution to the riddle of dear, old, good, industrious Frau Wachtel from before.

Being nature's livery, or fortune's star, whichever it was, the little prince of Norway was lying there, blithely, spacious in his possession.

IV

Since the beautiful sewer inspector's wife, carefully sewn into burlap, had finally been dispatched and none of the further promenades on the embankment had ever proven as productive, there was now nothing more to be had from little Ole Nissen next door. Nor did renewed attempts to gouge the great, fancy turkey come to fruition. His 'old lady' didn't seem to have impressed him much. In any case her little 'Tintoretto' had searched in vain for her on the new, beautifully wallpapered walls on his last official visit out there. Regretfully, the lady and gentleman of the house had just stepped out. It was not just in Christiania that they seemed ungrateful.

No more lobsters at Hiddersen's, no more Egyptian cigarettes, no more 'Kitty'! This last, of course, pained poor little Ole the most. But one couldn't really blame the little thing. Soggy bread crusts were not enough to sate anyone.

However, this came as a great relief to dear, good, old Frau Wachtel. For she had once caught the sweet little Kitty modelling for the hideous Ole, and since she really didn't have the slightest understanding for such things, she nursed a certain petty bias against her.

Unfortunately, she had seldom had occasion to put her good heart to use of late. In any case, it was the foolish Thienwiebels with whom she was most unsatisfied. It was not difficult to divine what would ultimately emerge from the mess up there.

The old fool lolled around on the sofa all day pulling faces, the lazy, consumptive wench didn't even have time to give her screaming tot a little blue milk, the three of them had nothing to eat between them, and the rent – oh, oh dear God! If only they had put a little aside …

– – Yes! It was wormwood! His wit was diseased! He lacked advancement! In the secret parts of fortune? O, most true! She is a strumpet! What's the news? When Roscius was still an actor in Rome … Arm'd, say you? Very like! Very like! – A man that fortune's buffets and rewards hast ta'en with equal thanks, who was not a pipe for fortune's finger to sound what stop she please, beggar that he was … no more of it! Say on: come to Hecuba!

Indeed, it could no longer be denied: he really was now pitiable, the great Thienwiebel!

O, what a rogue and peasant slave was he!! Was it not monstrous? Was it to be believed? Was it possible? Was it some habit that too much o'er-leavens the form of plausive manners, was it the o'ergrowth of some com-plexion: in short, but now he kept coming back to it: to nothing, to Hecuba!

What should such fellows as he do crawling between earth and heaven? Compounded it with dust, whereto 'tis kin, thus be-netted round with villanies … not so, my lord! The Mouse-trap? Marry, how? Tropically! I pray thee, do not mock me, fellow-student; I think it was to see my mother's wedding!

Poor Yorick! For if the sun breed maggots in a dead dog, being a god kissing carrion … Poor Yorick!

His madness was poor Hamlet's enemy. –

Amalie, who had at last made good on her threat and had indeed for some time been doing what she called sewing jersey bodices, confidently let it all wash over her.

It was no use! It didn't matter! Either way.

The good little Ole Nissen was infinitely more sensitive. As Frau Wachtel had recently been so kind as to take his fine liverwurst-coloured trousers to the pawnbroker like so many other beloved items, he was now doomed to lie in bed all day and listen to the entire household through the thin wooden walls.

'O! Villany! Go, let the door be lock'd! Treachery! Seek it out! Thou pray'st not well! I prithee! Take thy fingers from my throat! Dost know this water-fly?!'

Poor little Ole! Was it fear or merely boredom? But his forehead often broke out in drops of sweat.

The great Thienwiebel seemed to have him in his sights! In fact, he never failed to inspect his 'den' every afternoon at five o'clock sharp. Admittedly it was even more wretched than his own, but it did offer the advantage that you could easily climb out of the window onto the broad, flat, tarred roof below, from which you could enjoy a delightful view of the silent firewalls of several rear blocks. There was a small, unprepossessing plum tree, whose stunted branches were teeming with caterpillars and sparrows, to complete the idyll. Poor little Ole always felt this fateful hour in his bones long before it struck. For the great Thienwiebel would always engage him in conversations that were so ingenious, so full of ideas and so rich in colour that poor little Ole, already beleaguered by his eternal bread crusts, would always come away with a throbbing head.

'Sir, I will walk here in the hall: if it please his majesty, 'tis the breathing time of day with me. Let the foils be brought!'

The 'foils' were two pieces of a ladder that could be put together and hooked into the window frame from outside.

Once they had been 'brought' the episode always ended, of course, with them actually hanging them and using them to climb down.

'Hic et ubique! Then we'll shift our ground!'

Then they were in 'Elsinore', promenading on the 'platform'. The great Thienwiebel in fez and dressing gown, little Ole in his havelock and drawers.

'I will requite your loves. So, fare you well, Horatio! Upon the platform, 'twixt eleven and twelve, I'll visit you … won't I? You … are a – fishmonger?!'

O shame! where was thy blush?

In the end poor little Ole didn't know himself any more: whether he was really crazy, or Nielsie.

But he needn't have been so concerned. The great Thienwiebel knew only too well what he was doing. He was merely 'mad with method'. He was but mad north-north-west; when the wind was southerly he could very well distinguish a church tower from a lamppost.

The endless nude modelling down there in the old, stupid academy had lately become well-nigh tedious to him, and as dear, good, old Frau Wachtel was hardly likely to house him gratis for much longer if he now, *sans façon*, plugged this 'source of delicious ducats' up again, one fine day he fell upon the grand idea of slowly pretending to be truly mad here in this harsh world.

'Hillo! Ho, ho, boy! Come, bird! Come! I must to England; you know that? Heaven and earth! It is but foolery; but it is such a kind of omen, as would perhaps trouble a woman. How now! A rat? The point!–envenom'd too? No! No, fair lady! 'Tis not alone my inky cloak, good mother, nor customary suits of solemn black, nor windy suspiration of forced breath, no: the mattering unction, too! I have sworn 't! I'll wipe away all trivial fond records from the table of my memory! Never crook the pregnant hinges of the knee where thrift may follow fawning! We defy augury: there's a special providence in the fall of a sparrow. The readiness is all. 'Sblood! Do you think I am easier to be played on than a pipe? Call me what instrument you will! Though you can fret me, yet you cannot play upon me …'

Hillo! How now! A *royal* boyish knave!

Little Fortinbras appeared utterly unimpressed by this royal boyish knave. Indeed, certain signs sometimes led his big papa to conclude that he hadn't even taken proper notice of him.

This was most apparent when it came to the 'rudiments of vocal artistry'. For 'poor Yorick' was by no means willing, for the sake of his terrible madness, to let the rare talents of his son, who warranted such high hopes, wither away.

It was agreed! It was agreed, o fair Ophelia! Yes! Let's tell Ophelia! Devil! Why should we not tell Ophelia? In short: it was agreed. Him and his cause were to be reported aright to the unsatisfied … The unsatisfied! …

As soon as there was an indication that little Ole next door had gone back to sleep and good Frau Wachtel had gone out again and thus 'the two whom I will trust as I will adders fang'd' had been rendered 'harmless' for a time, the dance began.

At once the 'trappings and suits' of his woe seemed to have fallen away from the great Thienwiebel.

His 'imaginations, as foul as Vulcan's stithy' had left poor Yorick, he was once again 'tame, sir!'

'Hear you! I am tame again, sir: pronounce! I am tame again!'

But the stubborn little Fortinbras would not. In the absence of his rubber teat which the fair Ophelia had lost, he had once again stuffed his big toe into his mouth and was now sucking so hard on it that he was salivating from the corner of his small, dull rose mouth. The rudiments of vocal artistry apparently left him even colder than usual on this day.

Now the great Thienwiebel had reared up again in indignation. Naturally he had forgotten to tie the two red tassels on the back of his dressing gown.

'Amalie! I have just noticed to my great astonishment that Fortinbras is obstinate!'

Amalie, who to her great dismay had been forced to move her plump little footstool from the stove to the window because of the jersey bodices, was just about to thread her first needle for the day. She had had to inhale for so long again …

'Obstinate?'

'I'm telling you, Amalie! Obstinate!'

'Oh stop it!'

'Amalie? I tell you again – obstinate! Fortinbras is obstinate! Obs-ti-nate!!'

'Oh, don't say that! What's obstinate about him!'

'Amalie?!'

Amalie didn't even turn around. She barely shrugged.

'Oh! Oh! So you no longer believe me when I tell you something! You distrust me! Indeed! Indeed! I might have known! Why not come out with it! Why cavil! You're sorry that I don't wear myself out any faster!'

Amalie sneezed. She just could not get rid of her cold. In the middle of summer.

'Naturally! How could you not! You spend your time – sneezing! You drink coffee and spend your time – sneezing! Indeed! Indeed! Other people might just let themselves go to ground! … But I will prove it to you, Amalie! Do you hear? I will prove to you that Fortinbras is obstinate! – – You! Say *ah* … *ah* … Well? Come on! … Well? … *Ah!* … You rogue! *Ah!* … *Ah!!* … Ha! Do you see?! Just as I told you, just as I told you, Amalie! The tyke roars as if his head were off! He is obstinate! Was I right?! – Will you be quiet, you zebra?! I'll make you quiet!'

Finally Amalie had suddenly become a little more attentive at her window.

'Surely you aren't going to – hit him?'

'Certainly I am, Amalie! A child must not be headstrong! A child needs bringing up, Amalie! A light castigation …'

'Niels!?'

'What then? Out of the way! Get out of the way, I say! … There, you great rogue! There, you gr – … Amaaalie!'

'Indeed, you old ass! You think you can just do whatever you please here? You ought to be in an insane asylum! How can you abuse a six-month-old child like that?! How can you beat him!'

'Amaaalie!!'

Was it possible?! Was it to be believed?! Was that his cheek?!

'Amaaalie!!! …'


V


'Thrift! Thrift, Horatio! The funeral baked meats did coldly furnish forth the marriage tables. Er – yet, but, in the beaten way of friendship, what make you at Elsinore?'

The great Thienwiebel had to stay in the beaten way of friendship again; what was little Ole supposed to be doing in Elsinore? What he had been doing for weeks: painting shop signs! 'You know it's paying off splendidly!'

Abel Gröndal: fabric store, and herrings as well – Lars Brodersen: canary seeds and hemp seeds – Jacob Lorrensen: all manner of smoking, snuff and chewing tobacco – and so on and so forth. Huh?! Well?! Great turkeys!!

He was parading around in his fine liver-wurst-coloured trousers once again, the splendid Egyptian cigarettes were puffed away by the pound again, the devilish little Kitty barely gave poor, dear, good old Frau Wachtel a moment's rest from the keyhole.

But truly, it was awful the things one could see in there now. The myriad white ointment pots into which the paints were squeezed like butter, the outsized masonry brushes which busy little Ole was barely able to manage, the fine, thick, boards as tall as a man on which one could now read the most wondrous things and, above all, the large, mysterious, green screen close to the stove, behind which the shameful little Kitty was always hiding, all of this was of the most vivid interest to old, dear, good Frau Wachtel. She had never felt so satisfied with her position of landlady. The most pressing of the old arrears were paid off, she no longer had to fret so about the dozy Thienwiebels, yes, yes! Dear Lord!

The fair Ophelia had fallen back into her old stupor. She regretted her misdeed most profoundly. The only thing left in her life was her sage pot.

Her great husband simply despised her now … Written – er … they had already written to him, but – er … why were they roaming about? A fixed abode was more beneficial to their reputation than their income! In short, it was just a touring company, and the great Thienwiebel had feared lowering himself. As long as little Ole was still there next door … in short: he did whatever profession and inclination dictated! Because … er … everyone has an inclination and a profession!

However, the one who fared worst was most certainly little Fortinbras. His little teeth had completely ruined his nice rubber teat. He took no joy in anything any more; not even screaming.

He had become a consummate pessimist. As for his future profession, explaining his great father to the unsatisfied, that seemed to matter very little to him now. His little tongue was thickly coated, his little hands looked as white as cake batter, he often slept for whole days now.

Only on this evening was he noticeably lively.

The two bright lamps on the table, the crowd of people, the uproar, the strangely large sugar pretzel that had been put in his hand so unexpectedly: he didn't understand any of it. Just more powder!

The ladies had taken their places on the sofa, little Kitty, who counted herself among the menfolk, was sitting opposite little Ole, the great Thienwiebel presided. The magnificent goose in the middle of the table, into whose sumptuous, crispy back he had just vigorously thrust his gleaming carving fork, filled the little room with its aroma. The two lamps on the right and left burned through their steam as though through a fog. Frau Wachtel, who felt as through she were on a platter in her corner of the sofa, was breathing heavily. She was wearing her 'silk ensemble' today.

'Masters, you are all welcome. We'll e'en to't like French falconers, fly at any thing we see. By heaven! I'll make a ghost of him that lets me! … Ha! Are you honest??'

'Thienwiebel, dear?'

Little Ole, who had just got stuck into his sumptuous wing, blinked with delight. Little Kitty looked good enough to eat again today!

'Thienwiebel dear?!'

The charming little dimple in her pink little finger was displayed to full effect.

'Thienwiebel dear? There is something!'

But the great Thienwiebel, who had now stuffed the napkin under his blue double chin, felt himself quite abreast of the situation.

'Do you think I have edifying things on my mind? A fine thought, between the …'

'Nielsie!!'

Little Ole believed his time had come.

He had now poured himself his splendid port and swung it cheerfully towards the new lamp.

'Turkey number 25!'

His fine jubilee was not going to turn to water in a hurry.

'Turkey number 25!'

Little Kitty was quite flushed with pleasure now. The two little silver rings flashed in her earlobes, her little snub nose looked like marzipan.

'Bravo, dumpling! Live it up! Turkey number 25!'

She had toasted him boisterously.

Frau Wachtel was now clearing her throat. Her silk ensemble had just got caught on something.

'Would you like – some gravy perhaps, Frau Thienwiebel?'

Amalie nodded. Her plate was already swimming, but: it didn't matter. Either way.

Her great husband was over there trying to get into the part again.

'Well, well, fair lady! For – er – if the sun breed maggots in a dead dog, being a deity … Ha! Rebellious hell! What is he whose grief bears such an emphasis?!'

It was little Fortinbras. His sugar pretzel had just fallen over the rim of the basket onto the edge of the chair, where it now lay broken in two and crumbled into small pieces on the dirty floorboards.

'Ha, thou incestuous, murderous, damned Dane!

Drink off this potion! I'll lug the guts into the neighbour room!'

But little Kitty had quickly put her fork back on her plate, concerned.

'Oh! Not that, Thienwiebel dear! Not that!'

She had leapt up and was now bending delicately over the plump rim of the basket.

'Oh my sweet little dolly! My treasure! Such a bonny little fellow! You want something too, don't you? Oh, my little sweetheart!'

She now had little Fortinbras on her lap and was kissing him, just like that.

'You want something too, dumpling?' Kiss! – 'You want something too, dumpling?' Kiss! Kiss, kiss, kiss, kiss!!

Little Fortinbras crowed. In all his days he had never known the like. He was fidgeting most noisily now. He was laughing out loud!

'Grrr … grrr … grrr … ay! Grrr … ay!'

The great Thienwiebel sat there. His vest unbuttoned at the bottom, his eyebrows raised tragically.

'How bold the knave is! … By the Lord, Horatio! These three years I have taken a note of it. The age is grown so picked that the toe of the peasant comes so near the heel of the courtier, he gaffs his kibe!'

But little Ole barely noticed him. He was far more interested in little Kitty now. At that moment she looked like a proper mater familias.

'Well, dumpling?'

Even Frau Wachtel's eyes widened now. Amalie mopped.

'Yes, my lad! All of them eating, and my little dumpling has none! What? – But he isn't at all happy about that! What? – Oh, please, Frau Thienwiebel! Hand me that piece of biscuit from the dresser. The milk too, please!'

Frau Thienwiebel got up sluggishly and brought what was requested.

Little Kitty had softened the biscuit and was now starting to feed little Fortinbras with it. She barely nibbled from her plate, which held nothing more than a few small bits of greasy skin alongside the three roasted apples.

Little Fortinbras groaned with pleasure.

'Well? Do you want more, little dumpling? Even more?'

Little Ole had now bent over the edge of the table in curiosity. His moustache smelled of Chinese ink.

'No! No! Just look, little dumpling! Doesn't he love it! – What?! – Even more?! – No! No! Just don't start screaming! – There!'

Frau Wachtel was now properly moved to tears. And whenever she was moved to tears, she never failed to talk about her late foster daughter. And that happened quite often.

'Yes, you see! She was an angel, Frau Thienwiebel! An angel!'

Frau Thienwiebel chewed.

Frau Wachtel now described in detail the angel's illness and how she then died. Little Mala they called her, and she had been so divinely patient.

'Yes, you see, Herr Nissen! She was my one and

only! She was still comforting me when death came. She was an angel!'

She had now remembered her handkerchief and was dabbing it at each eye in turn.

'Oh, do not weep, Mother! Do not weep! Now I am going to the Lord God!'

She was weeping so much now that her tears rolled down her silk ensemble!

Little Ole had been shifting sheepishly back and forth in his chair for some time. He was aiming for the sweet little foot under the table and had just stumbled upon the old, phlegmatic felt slippers of the fair Ophelia.

It made him turn quite red.

'Yes! You see! She was my one and only!'

Little Fortinbras thrashed about in delight.

'Grrr … grrr … grrr …'

That friendly, fresh face with the bright eyes and the blond curls above him – he couldn't stop laughing! He had even forgotten about his powder!

'Grrr … grrr … grrr … aaeee!'

His little hands were now grasping the air above him, the little Kitty let him ruffle her curls.

'No, little dumpling! Look, don't touch!'

Little Ole blew his nose. He was now entirely blood red.

'Yes! I believe you! You haven't had it this good before, dumpling! Well?'

Now Frau Wachtel was finally bending over him too. Her handkerchief was once again neatly folded out on her lap, she tickled him sympathetically under his chin.

'Oh, my little cherub! Oh, my mouse! Have they

been starving you for so very long!'

Her voice trembled, she still looked quite tearful.

Amalie was dunking in her gravy.

The great Thienwiebel, however, had leaned back in his chair with his hands in his trouser pockets and was now staring grandly at the two yellow dabs of light that the lamps were tremulously painting on the ceiling.

Because, what so poor a man as Hamlet is ... no more of it!

The rest was silence ...

Finally everything was cleared away again. Frau Wachtel, who did not play cards, had retreated back to her kitchen with her silk ensemble, her handkerchief and her second lamp; Amalie was crouching on her footstool next to the stove once again. She had helped herself to bread and dripping.

It was quite cold in the room. The fire had gone out and there was nothing more to add to it. The great Thienwiebel, whose dressing gown was no longer fit for cards, had instead wrapped himself in the red bedspread.

'The air bites shrewdly; it is very cold! Tourner, Horatio!'

'Passez, Nielsie!'

'Ditto, Tiensie!'

'What is it, little lamb?'

'Get a move on!'

'Ah yes! – There, little lamb!'

'Finally!'

She had taken the cigarette that little, avid Ole had given her and was holding it with her fingertips, and she now made a face as though the smoke were bothering her. She knew that it became her! It also had the immediate success of her dumpling pilfering a kiss.

'Leave it! What a nerve!'

She had knocked him under the table with her knee.

'Ace of spades! Isn't that right, Wiebel dear?'

'Very good, fair lady! Very good! Excellent, in good faith! Why, what should be the fear? I – er – I am myself – er – hmmm! – indifferent honest …'

Little Fortinbras was now entirely forgotten.

'Full of bread with all his crimes broad blown, as flush as May,' he was now once again 'safely stowed' back in his dark basket and was staring gloomily into the cigar smoke that billowed in thick layers around the green dome. He had not often ventured out of his corner since he was born. His unexpected fortune today had made him long for the light there. The lap, the sugar pretzel, the curls … he had begun to mewl again.

Amalie didn't stir. The rascal just wanted to be picked up all the time. Once was enough for her.

'Hearts are trumps, Nielsie!'

'What did you say?'

'I said: hearts are trumps, Nielsie! Hearts are trumps!'

'Ha, bloody, bawdy villain! It's impossible to understand a word with this accursed screaming! If you are not quiet immediately, you disgraceful brat, I shall strike you as blue as a blueberry!'

'Oh no! You're pinching, Ole! Ouch!'

'Oh what, little lamb! Leave it be!'

The sofa was more than preoccupied with itself

at that moment.

Amalie, who was already half dozing on her little footstool again, barely blinked. The great Thienwiebel was safe from a second slap.

He had planted himself angrily before the basket in his red bedspread and was now roaring angrily at the poor little bundle.

'Will you be quiet, you – scallywag!?'

But it wasn't the 'scallywag'. He wanted to go all in as well. He was now screaming fit to burst his little lungs.

'But ... now this is outrageous! ... Just you wait! You ... you – lindworm, you! Just wait!'

He beat him now, slapping him, just like that. But when that didn't help either, he pulled the pillow out from under him and pressed it to his face.

Little Fortinbras fell completely silent in an instant. It was as though his screams were cut off.

But it still wasn't enough for the great Thienwiebel.

'Useless individual!'

He had pressed the pillow even more firmly on him now.

Little Ole had let go of the little Kitty, who was still quite red with anger. He was now truly fearful.

'For God's sake, Nielsie! He's suffocating!'

'Nonsense! It doesn't happen that quickly!'

No! It didn't happen that quickly! For when the great Thienwiebel took the pillow away after a while, the little Fortinbras desperately gasped for breath for a few moments, but then immediately started all over again.

'Ole!'

Little Kitty had leapt up, outraged. The terrible pillow was now covering the little one again.

'Ole! How can you put up with this?'

'Nonsense! He knows very well, the lout! He's not to scream! It is pure wickedness! One can get heartily sick of it!'

'Ugh! Ole, come! Leave the old – baboon!'

'Ba … ba … ba …'

Little Ole was now looking at his watch, embarrassed.

'… Baboon?!!!'

Finally the great Thienwiebel came to his senses!

'Out, I say!! Out!'

But they already were. For a moment he heard them groping out there through the kitchen; then, finally, the adjacent door had slammed.

He stood there! The red bedspread around his shoulders and the small, blue checked cushion in his right hand. Over there, in the stove corner, fair Ophelia.

'There! Nymph!!'

He had thrown the pillow in her face. –


VI


Dear, good, old Frau Wachtel hadn't had so much trouble since her disagreeable second husband had faithlessly departed for Canada on the 'Fat Selma'.

It wasn't just that the heels of his boots could still be clearly seen all over the sofa, it wasn't just that the window crossbar was totally ruined by the stupid ladder pieces that now, naturally, lay broken down on the sheeting roof: the whole wallpaper was stained from top to bottom with oil paint! The accursed titchy filthmonger seemed to have spent his entire time squeezing his horrible brush out on it. Devil take him!

But she was glad to see him gone! Why had she not thrown the whole lot of them out on the street long ago! If only it had been the lunatic Thienwiebels. But Satan wouldn't take them! They were hooked onto her like burrs!

Old, dear, good Frau Wachtel was completely beside herself. But she had truly rotten luck with her menfolk. Little Ole even had the effrontery to run away and leave behind some old 'daubs' whose subjects made it impossible to hang them over the sofa.

'Such an act that blurs the grace and blush of modesty, calls virtue hypocrite, takes off the rose from the fair forehead of an innocent love and sets a blister there … Ha!'

But the great Thienwiebel now tried in vain to make himself popular. His 'mattering unction' no longer worked. Frau Rosine Wachtel was now emphatically demanding her rent.

Today was the seventh: if she didn't receive everything by the fourteenth: – out!

Yes! … To die – to sleep – no more! And by a sleep to say we end the heart-ache and the thousand natural shocks that flesh is heir to – , 'tis a consummation devoutly to be wish'd! … Yes! this was before the paradox! Paradox! … But now – time confirmed it! Poor Yorick! …

The great Thienwiebel now felt that his strength

was at an end. He wanted to work now, friend! Work! He wanted to summon all his strength. He – he … he wanted to go 'looking'! 'Leave me! He is murdered, Amalie! He is murdered!' …

He had patched up his old, olive-green frock coat again and was now drifting around the port quarter all day long. – 'Ha! Dead?! For a ducat, dead?!' … He had another great excuse. A boyish knave! Now he barely needed to go home at night. He got by as best he could. There were still – er: colleagues! People! People? Pah, bunglers! But – er … they – er … Well, yes! They saw the players well bestowed! 'Sblood! There was something in this more than natural! If only philosophy could find it out! …

But philosophy did not find it out. The great Thienwiebel never did figure it out.

Bit by bit he had drifted, right down to the low taverns of the port. He was already on intimate terms with a number of stevedores. He seldom stumbled up the stairs before 'the cock, that is the trumpet to the morn' had crowed several times.

Amalie was still sewing her jersey bodices. The stupor had gradually made a mere machine of her. The fair Ophelia in her was now finally buried. For all time! … Her chest had become even weaker …

The condition of little Fortinbras was even more pitiable. His whole face was now dabbed with red pustules. A little box of zinc salve, acquired when the family still ran to such things, was now squeezed out and covered with dust behind the stove. It had not been replaced.

The great Thienwiebel was not entirely wrong: the whole household at home was the abstract and brief chronicle of the time.


VII

Twelve! …

Exhausted, she had sunk back on her footstool. The stove behind her was ice-cold. She could clearly feel its tiles through her nightshirt. She was shivering!

From outside the last chimes hummed and trembled, on the upturned box before her the small tallow candle that had been placed in an empty, green beer bottle in the middle of her sewing crinkled in the cold.

Frau Wachtel next door was snoring, little Fortinbras had restlessly rolled onto his other side in his basket. His breath rattled, in fits and starts, as though something inside him had broken.

Another icicle had just clattered on the window sill. Right before it, the sharp gnawing of a mouse was now clearly audible from under the bed.

Twelve!

She had dropped her sewing again. Her fingers were bent together, she could hardly prise them open. They were blue around the nails. She breathed into them now. Her breath seethed dusty grey around the small, trembling flame. A late fly that had fallen into the small, round tallow pot beneath the black wick slowly charred. Now and then it crackled . . . . . . . . . . . . . . . . . . . . . . . . .
. . . . . . . . . . . . . . . . . . . . . . . . . . . . . . . . . . . .

'Grab him! Grab him! Help!! Help!!'

She had shuddered, alarmed.

Now she looked up. Her slack, white face had become even more vacant.

'Here! Here! Help!!'

The yellow blob of light before her now made the room behind it appear even darker. Only the dull snowy light from outside through the window and the angular hole in the bedspread.

'Help! Help!!'

She had leapt up and rushed to the window. The little tallow candle behind her had gone out. It had fallen over and was now under the sewing.

'Watchman!! Watchman!! Grab him!! Jonas! Jonas!!'

Trembling in every limb she had now pulled the old bedspread up and was trying to see down to the street below through the whirling snowflakes. Her teeth chattered with frost, the scissors that she still held tightly in her hand clinked against the pane in time.

A few gables stood out blue-grey across the way in the darkness. Somewhere a light flickered in a window.

'Hooray! Papa Svendsen! Hello, old boy! Happy New Year!!'

She breathed a sigh of relief. There was loud laughter. Now: a harsh voice, a stick that quickly rattled down another shutter, the whole group had turned the corner again.

For a little while she listened.

Now and then the sound of snow tumbling from roofs, in the distance, softly, a sleigh bell.

She had dropped the blanket again. –

She stood there for a moment! The whole room was black now. Only the snowy light behind her, dulled by the blanket.

She padded over to the table.

She hit the edge. A bottle had tipped over, it smelled of spirits. The matchbox had rustled now, it flickered! It shone across the table. The narrow gold rim around the small photograph glittered. The night lamp stood on the old, splayed book in the middle of the dishes.

Now a faint spray and crackling, the wick had caught light. Above her, looming against the ceiling, her shadow.

Frau Wachtel next door was snoring, little Fortinbras groaned.

She was now on the edge of the bed. She pressed the two tips of the pillow that she had wrapped around her shoulders firmly against her chest with her chin. Her arms had cramped against her body, her drawn up knees were pressed tightly together. She was trembling all over! Her face was contorted and she was staring apathetically. The scissors that had tipped off the table earlier lay before her on the grey floorboards. She blinked.

The lamp on the table had now started to tremble slightly, the bright, elongated circles that its liquid had cast across the ceiling and a piece of wallpaper swayed. The dishes around the glass stood out black from them. The coffee pot reached right over the ceiling.

'Brrr … Ach!'

Her slippers had now flown under the table, she

had huddled hastily under the bedcover.

The white rings of light flooded, flooded, the oil on the table crackled softly, a small spark had just spurted off its wick and was now floating black in the thick, golden-yellow mass.

There was a lump beneath the bedcover over there now. At one spot her petticoat peeped out . . . . . . . . . . . .

'Quiet, hound! … Ach!!'

He had now torn his old top hat, still covered in thick snow, from his head and flung it furiously into the dark, screaming corner where the basket was. The door behind him had slammed shut.

'Niels!!'

The bedcover, which was now lying across the floorboards, had half swept the chair with it. She knelt upright in the middle of the bed. The front of her night-shirt had moved up under her arms, her hair hung in strands around her face.

'Shut your mouth! Don't you start too!'

He had now pulled off his old, shabby coat too. The little mirror above the dresser against which he had thrown it had been cast down and now lay splintered on the blinking growth.

'Well, get a move on!'

Little Fortinbras just gasped.

'Well?! … Your luck, scoundrel! …'

His boots had now thumped against the small box by the stove. Caked snow came off them and now splashed wet against the tiles. He was now looking for his slippers.

'Oh what is it! Shut your mouth, I say! … Blaring in my ears … Just what I needed! … Is everything packed?!'

The snoring next door had stopped. There was a conspicuous rubbing against the door now.

'Have you packed?!'

'No, Niels … I …'

She stuttered!

'Of course not! You have consumption again for a change! … Please don't be shy, Frau Wachtel! Come closer! It's all happening today!'

His shadow, which until then was shooting back and forth across the white ceiling, had now disappeared. He had bent down under the table.

A loud coughing had just started up from the bed.

'Oh, my dear God! … Oh God! Oh God! The poor woman!'

She had now pressed her face into the pillow and was crying.

'Go on! Go on! Now sob a little! That's your forte! And that's all you can do!'

He had just put his slippers on and was now looking around on the table. A knife clattered against the range, a cup had overturned.

'Of course! Not a scrap left! For a consumptive you've certainly got a healthy appetite! … Wonderful! It always acts as if it sucks on air and it eats the hair off your head!'

He had stuffed his fists in his trouser pockets and was snorting up and down the room.

'What a pack! What a – pack!!'

He had kicked the small, empty box with the sewing. The bottle had hit the floor and the light rolled under the bed.

'Ridiculous!'

He had now pushed the bottle under too. 'Ridiculous!! … Will you be quiet?!!'

Little Fortinbras had started screaming loudly again.

'Beast!'

With one leap he was at the basket.

'Beast!!'

The screaming was cut off again.

'Stupid circus!'

He had turned back to the bed now. His fists were clenched. There was audible sobbing from under the pillows.

'Old crybaby!'

The two thick lines around his nose were deeper now, his wide teeth flashed between his twisted lips.

'Ach!!'

A shiver had run down his back.

'It's so cold!'

He was noisily shifting the chair into position.

'It's so cold!! There aren't even a few lumps of coal! What a household!'

He had pulled off his socks now, one of which had been cast to the middle of the table beneath the dishes.

'Well?! Would you be so good?!'

She pressed herself even further against the wall.

'Well! Finally!'

He had crawled under the covers with her now,

he had kept his drawers on.

'Not even enough room to sleep!'

He stretched his whole body.

'It's a dog's life! Can't even sleep!'

He had rolled over to the other side again. He had pulled the blanket off her shoulder as he turned, she lay there almost naked now . . . . . . . . . . . . . . . . . . . . . .
. . . . . . . . . . . . . . . . . . . . . . . . . . . .

The night lamp on the table had now stopped shaking.

The steamed-up blue carafe in front of it was studded with countless little spots of light. A page from the book had opened diagonally against the glass. In the middle of the yellowed paper the bold text stood out clearly: 'A Midsummer Night's Dream'. Behind it on the wall above the sofa, the small, glittering photograph cast its black, rectangular shadow.

Little Fortinbras rattled, there was snoring to be heard from next door again.

'What a life! What a life!'

He had turned back toward her. His voice was now soft, tearful.

'And you don't say anything!'

She simply sobbed again.

'Oh God, yes! Such a … Ach!! …'

He had now moved even closer to the edge.

'There's plenty of room there! Why are you pressed against the wall! You've no need!'

She shook. A stale brandy odour had gradually spread over the whole bed.

'What a life! We've really come a long way! …

Now to be kicked out by that old witch! Lovely!! Well, so what now? Out on the street tomorrow! … Will you say something?'

She was pressed even tighter against the wall now. Her sobs had stopped, she turned her back on him.

'I know! It's not your fault either! Say something!'

He had moved toward her again now.

'Say something! … We can't just – starve to death?!'

He was right behind her now.

'I can't help it either! … This isn't like me at all! It's true! It's this life – it turns you into a beast! … You're not asleep already, are you?'

She coughed.

'Oh God, yes! And now you're sick as well! And the child! All this sewing … But you're not taking care of yourself either … I tell you!'

She had started sobbing again.

'You – should – have – Niels …'

'Yes … Yes! I see it now! I should have accepted it! And I should have later on … I see it now! It was rash! I should have grabbed it! But – say something!!'

'Did you – if not … if not – at least – go and see him at home?'

'Oh God, yes, but … but you know! He has nothing either! What do we do now? We can't just end it all?!'

He had now started crying too.

'Oh God! Oh God!!'

His face was now in between her breasts. She twitched!

'Oh God! Oh God!!'

The dark rim of the glass above, across the ceiling, had begun to tremble restlessly again, the shadows cast by the dishes swayed, with ripples of water glittering between them . . . . . . . . . . . . . . . . . . . . . . . . . . . . . . . . . . . . . . . . . . . . . . . . . . .

'Oh not now, Niels! Not now! The child – is awake again! The – child is screaming! The – child, Niels … go and look! For God's sake!' Her elbows were now pressed firmly behind her on the pillows, her nightshirt was wide open at the front.

The dull gurgle over in the corner had broken out into something like a thin, hoarse bark. There was a scrabbling from the rags, the whole basket was creaking.

'Take a look!!'

'Of course! Just what I needed! The Devil take the brat! …'

He was now back in his slippers.

'You can't even rest at night! Not even the night any more!!'

The dishes on the table had started clinking again, the shadows swinging over the wall above. –

'Huh? You!! What is it now? Well? … Where is he? … Ach, what a pigsty!'

He had found the rubber teat and was now wiping it on his drawers.

'It's so cold! Well? Hurry up! Well? Take it, camel! Take it! Well?!'

Little Fortinbras gasped!

His little head had cramped into his neck, he was now pressing it desperately in every direction.

'Huh? Do you want it or not?! – – Beast!!'

'But – Niels! For God's sake! He's having an – attack again!'

'Nonsense! Attack! – There! Eat!!'

'Good God, Niels …'

'Eat!!!'

'Niels!' . . . . . . . . . . . . . . . . . . . . . . . . . . . .

'Huh? Will you be – quiet now? Well? – Will you be – quiet now? Well?! Well?!'

'Oh God! Oh God, Niels, what, what – are you doing?! He, he – he's not crying at all any more! He … Niels!!'

She had recoiled instinctively. His whole figure was crouched forward, his cracking fingers clenched crookedly in the rim of the basket. He stared at her. His face was ashen.

'The … l - amp! The … l - amp! The … l - amp!'

'Niels!!!'

She had stumbled back against the wall before him.

'Quiet! Quiet!! Is – is someone knocking?'

Her two hands were spread behind her flat against the wallpaper, her knees were shaking.

'Is – is someone knocking?'

He had crouched lower now. His shadow swung above him, his eyes suddenly looked white now.

A floorboard creaked, the oil crackled, the snow-melt dripped onto the gutter outside.

Drip . . . . . . . . . . . . . . . . . . . . . drip . . . . . . . .
. . . . . . . . . . . . drip . . . . . . . . . . . . drip . . . . . . . . . . . .

Eight days later, the little hunchbacked baker's boy Tille Topperholt was balancing his bread basket, whistling his way down the dark, snow-covered Severin Alley to the harbour. The weather had changed again, his little snub nose looked horribly blue.

'Hail, Svea! Mother to us all!'

It had just struck five. In front of the big new liquor store on the corner of the church of St Peter's, he stumbled. Jesus! His rolls had flown into the gutter, he had fallen in the middle of the snow. But he didn't even stop to pick them up. By the time he had come to his senses again he was already grabbing the big bell covered in thick ice over at Jakobi Square, which immediately alerted the whole police station upstairs. Jesus! Jesus!!

When fat Sieversen finally came trudging along, he verified that the man had frozen to death. 'Frozen from drink!' The little hunchbacked Tille had squashed his battered top hat against the lantern. The bottle was still peeking out from his ragged, apple-green waistcoat.

Well now, a dramatic speech!

It was the great Thienwiebel.

And his soul? His soul, that immortal thing?

In conclusion! Life is brutal, Amalie! Take my word for it! But – it didn't matter! Either way!

# A DEATH

Finally, now that old Svendsen had ceased his monotonous patrol down below, Olaf could no longer stay upright either.

The long nocturnal vigil, the sharp carbolic vapour that entirely filled the narrow, stuffy room, the subtle ticking of the pocket watch from the coffee table, the soft, tireless burble and snap as the oil consumed itself in the lamp, turned down low, his own blood which hummed in his ears and at times sounded like distant, thin bells: all of this numbed him!

He had now sunk even lower into the big old calico armchair next to the bed. The glittering liquid in the half-full glass next to him, which he tried in vain to focus on, blurred into an orange-coloured dab of light, which gradually turned bluish. Finally no more than a brownish-red spark remained, then that too was extinguished. Everything seemed black now! The glass, the bed, the lamp, the whole room …

His chin fell to his chest, he had fallen asleep.

… Thank God! He was awake again. It must have been a mouse!

His shadow, which was now long and oddly buckled over the low white door up to the small, blue patch of wallpaper above it and the old, smoke-stained ceiling, brought him back into himself.

He checked his watch.

Three!

The patient was still lying there as though he were dead.

He had now bent over him.

The dull light from the bright red lamp traced the eye socket next to his sharp nose like a deep, sharp-edged hole in his skull.

'Poor chap!'

Once he had adjusted the large, damp towel across his forehead again, he fell back into his armchair once more.

'Poor chap!'

And once again, there was nothing but the soft, tireless burbling of the lamp, the ticking of the watch and Jens, who had turned over on his side as he slept on the old, rickety sofa …

Olaf sighed.

The dirty yellow patch of light on the old, cracked ceiling trembled, trembled, the watch ticked, his blood hummed, he had fallen asleep once more.

'O … Oolaf!!'

Down below, somewhere in the deathly quiet courtyard, some cats had just let out ear-splitting shrieks;

now Jens too was startled.

'For God's sake! What …'

'Stop that racket! … Those damn beasts!'

He was now wide awake again.

Jens yawned.

'Ha … huh! I … I think I – fell asleep for a bit!'

He had picked up the pince-nez that had slipped onto the sofa and was now pressing it back onto his snub nose.

'Hmmm!'

'Any better?'

'No! He's still sleeping!'

'Hmmm!'

For a while all was quiet once more. Even the cats outside had calmed down for a moment. Now Jens checked his watch. It had stopped.

'Three! Isn't it?'

'Yes! Only!!'

'Wonderful! … Do we still have beer?'

'Yes! I think so.'

Jens went to check. His thick felt socks made his footsteps inaudible. He stood for a moment by the bedside.

'Hey! Maybe he'll get better after all!'

Olaf just shrugged his shoulders.

One … two … three … five left.

'Do you want one too?'

'No! Thanks!'

'Aah! just what I needed! – By the way … the air's horribly stuffy in here!'

'Yes! You could cut it with a knife!'

'Terrible! Terrible!'

He was now standing before the window with both hands in his trouser pockets.

'Those damned animals!'

Olaf, who had been rummaging for a while through the small, red-lit bookshelf above the dresser, looked up.

'Yes! God knows! All night long!'

Jens now looked out onto the courtyard. He had pulled the curtains aside.

The two windows had cast their dim rectangles of light on the dark wall across the courtyard, up on a chimney the black silhouettes of two cats stood out sharply against the blue night sky. Two, three little stars flickered wearily above the roofs, which were covered with a soft grey light.

'Tegnér? Hmmm! Well! It doesn't matter anyway!'

Suddenly they both turned around uneasily.

A clear, sharp crack had gone through the deathly quiet room.

'No! … No! … It was just the stupid wardrobe again!'

'I thought … hmmm! As long as it doesn't come back again!'

Jens had involuntarily exhaled deeply.

He had now thrown his entire length across the sofa again.

Olaf had moved the Tegnér right under the small, old-fashioned lamp, around the cloche of which was a large, yellow sheet of newspaper, its corner reaching down to the table.

The pages crinkled in his hands. Raising his elbow, he now read aloud in a soft voice.

'Fair shines the sun, and from its rays of glory,
From bough to bough the gentle glitter leaps!'

The leaves crinkled again. The furrow between his thick, bushy eyebrows had dug itself even deeper.

Jens, who was now lying on his stomach over the arm of the sofa, watching the little green star over the chimney between the arabesques of the curtains, was horribly bored.

'Wouldn't you rather sleep a little?'

'No!'

'But child! … Why not? I'll take over!'

'Leave off! … Can't sleep!'

'Ach! Really! Me neither!'

There was a long silence. The two stared straight ahead, dulled and tired.

'Hey!'

'What?'

'Nothing!'

'What is it?'

'Quiet! Can't you hear something?!'

There was something scratching at the front door down in the hall.

'Aha!'

Jens returned to squinting sleepily up at his star.

'Hmmm!'

Olaf kept turning the pages.

In the meantime there was the sound of a key

in the lock downstairs, now being turned with difficulty. Someone staggered in.

'Hey! Listen to that!'

'Huh? Oh, goddamit!'

There was now a heavy stomping on the stairs. Whoever it was held on to the railing. At certain points the feet stumbled back a few steps. There was snorting and spluttering. A deep, hoarse bass voice hummed. Now, finally, there was a lumbering down the hall. A fat body thumped against a door. A truncated curse, then it continued on again.

'Holy cow!'

Jens laughed softly.

Now there was a bracing against the wall, scrabbling along it. A few pieces of plaster crumbled away and pattered onto the floorboards beneath.

'What?! Great toad!'

'Quiet!!'

It was coming … yes! … it was actually coming … to the door?

Now … It had crashed right into it! The dull thud went through the whole room.

'Good God! Who's this great oaf?!!'

Olaf shot straight up.

For Jens, too, the situation had become a little lively …

They were both standing in the middle of the room now, their eyes carefully fixed on the door.

There was a groping at the handle.

'That means …'

Olaf had now walked towards the door, quickly,

on the tips of his toes.

But it had already crashed open in the same moment and a misshapen, black lump barrelled over the threshold and into the room.

The cool breeze had caused the small lamp by the bed to flare up.

Jens had jumped straight away.

With Olaf's help, he finally managed to pull the drunkard up.

In the dull glow of the lamp there was now a blue-red, puffy face gawking stupidly around the room with its small, blurry eyes. Under his crushed hat against thin, flax-blonde hair on his red, fat, sweat-drenched forehead.

'Sir! This way!'

A gulp and a sniff was the sole response.

'You made a wrong turn!'

'Wha … hbf … wha … what? Hbf! …'

'You made a wrong turn!'

'Ah! … En … en … hbf! … shou … the … I … hbf! … I …'

'This way!'

'Hb! Hbf! …'

The fat man had stumbled backwards into the hallway with a bow. Olaf pressed the door firmly and turned the key …

'Fine household here!'

At last they had calmed down again.

Olaf leafed absent-mindedly through his Tegnér once more, Jens had thrown himself back on the sofa and was squinting sleepily through the curtain again.

At the head of the bed, from some corner came the sleepy hum of a fly roused by the light.

The pocket watch ticked, the sound of a few woodworms from the cupboard. Now, up on the third floor, the door finally slammed shut.

Through the thin ceiling came the clear sounds of a body falling clumsily onto a bed …

The dull, pale light up on the roofs had now turned a little brighter …

Olaf shook. He was shivering with cold. He turned the lamp wick up a little. The sick man's sharp, deathly pale face, with his damp black hair matted against his moist forehead beneath the towel, was now outlined even more sharply.

'Oh God, yes!'

Olaf had wearily put his head on his arms, which he had propped against the edge of the table.


Suddenly they both started in fright!

This time the creak was clearly coming from the bed.

A restless murmur. A groan. There was a leaden thud on the bulky blanket.

The two stared breathlessly …

'Ah! … aaah!! …'

Olaf had quickly bent over the sick man.

'Jens! Jens!'

'Here!'

The patient had now become even more restless. His head turned in all directions. His deep, dark eyes were wide open. His nails scratched sharply at the bed cover. His pale, bluish lips moved.

'Hey! Come here!'

'Yes!'

But he lay motionless again. Only his long, haggard hands tugged restlessly at the blanket. For a few seconds all was quiet …

Now, barely audible:

'Water …'

'Quick! Quick!'

'Here!'

Olaf had leaned over the bed again with the glass. Carefully, quietly, he pushed his long, sinewy arm under the patient's head. He cautiously lifted him up a little and pressed the glass to his mouth …

The sick man had drunk greedily! His eyes were now madly fixed on the dirty yellow trembling circle up on the whitewashed low crossbeam of the ceiling …

The soft, trembling clatter of the empty glass that Jens put back on the table, and the pocket watch nearby.

'H … h… go! Let's be off!!'

'Hey! Hey!'

'Yes!'

'Places! Aim! Fire!!! … Ah! … here! Here! In my side! … Ah! Aaah! … It hurts! It hurts, Olaf! Olaf! … hoo! The blood! The blood! … All the grass … aaah! … All the – grass … All the grass …'

Jens shook. It ran through him.

Olaf had now bent even lower over the bed.

'Martin! Martin! Old boy!'

His voice was trembling a little.

'Jens! a fresh cloth!' …

'Here!'

'Ah … the grass is … wet! … cool … so cool … We have to go, Olaf … The cab … down below … Quiet, child! Quiet! We have to make the chap believe it!! – Hold up! Hold up! The postman? Flinsberg, old chap! Not a shilling more, on my word! … money! Money! But Mother sent … Mother! … But it will be hard for her, Olaf! … Just don't tell … don't tell! Here, doctor! … Come in! … Wonderful! … the wheat … The birds … Oh, Doctor! … Leave me alone! … You don't need to hold me … I can do it myself … Stop! … Leave me alone!'

He writhed. Olaf had both arms wrapped around him now.

'No! Oh no! Let go, Jens! … Don't be stupid! Give me my briefcase! … I have to go to college! … Drink! Drink! … Throw the rest away! … Goddamit! Such a messy bout! … But … but … no, no! … Let me go! Let go!! Oh – just let go! Go!! … Silence! Let's have a song!'

His haggard arms were now thrashing wildly in the air. His slender hands dangled from his thin wrists.

Olaf groaned.

'We'll have a song! … The first song! … Page … No! … Go! … Go!! Let go – gooo!!!'

'Jens! Help … hold – him!'

'Go! Go!! – Gooo!!! … Let me go!! Let me go!! … Aah! Aaahh!!'

'Tight! – Tight!! … He's – trying – to get out!'

A board which had come loose under the old

bedstead had now crashed onto the floorboards. They were tossed back and forth …

Finally they had pushed Martin back into the rumpled bed. Now he was lying there, exhausted. He merely muttered to himself in a low voice. Jens had carefully rearranged the blanket that had been pulled down. They were both breathing hard …

A rooster was now crowing nearby.

'Ah! It hurts! It hurts so much!! Aah!! Aaaah!!! … Olaf! Olaf!!'

'Yes? My boy? … It's me! And Jens! … Are you feeling better?'

He had bent down to him again. His chest was still heaving. He could hardly speak.

'Yes! – Yes … So beautiful in the sun … Outside … This evening at Bergenhuus … on the beach … Isn't that right, Nora? … Oh, morning already … Just a frog! … Not really … just a frog … Here! Here! The grass is so beautiful … Oh, isn't it? We won't forget each other? … Never … never … Oh, never? … Another kiss? … hmmm? … Good night … The moon … so beautiful … there … over the lake … so red … so big … so biiiig …'

He lay there now, his eyes half closed. He smiled.

'He's calming down!'

'Yes …'

Olaf had now straightened up again. For a moment he had rubbed his arm. Jens wiped his forehead with the back of his hand.

'So cool … so beautiful … so …'

Olaf had straightened Martin's damp towel once again. Jens went over to the lamp.

'Four … only four … h! …'
He was now at the window again.
'If only it was day!'

The pale light outside on the roofs had now turned brighter. The first light of dawn lay dull golden yellow on the mossy dark red roof tiles and on the square chimney opposite. The narrow courtyard lay in dim silver-grey light. The breaking dawn crept slowly along the window niche into the musty room. The glossy leather of the sofa had begun to shimmer softly, the restless patch of light on the ceiling was growing paler. The wick of the lamp from which Olaf had removed the sheet of newspaper was now just a reddish, carbonised, stinking ring.

Outside the rooster crowed again. A faint gust of wind skimmed past the window. From the chimney of a neighbouring building fine, white smoke curled into the dull blue, square patch of sky above the rear blocks.

'When can they get here?'
'In two hours, I think!'
Jens had turned around again.
'Hey! Come here! – Quick!'

'No! No! … There is no point dawdling! Let's get to work now! Work!!'
'Hey!'
'Good God! Good God!'
He was now chatting softly to himself again.
Suddenly, at lightning speed, with an abrupt jolt, he sat straight up.
'Jens! … Quick! … Quick! … Do-own! Do-own!

The ban–dage!'

'Let's have a song!! … Let's have a song!!'

Martin sang …

His voice rang hoarse across the room.

'Tight! Hold on – tight!'

'Fttt!! That was an incommensurate blow! … Would the gentlemen please state without prejudice … h!! … h!! Here … Aaaahh!! …'

Martin was running both his hands over his body.

'Hold tight! For God's sake! … He's – tearing … the – bandage off!!'

Martin dashed.

'Hold on … as tight … as you – can!'

Jens struck his head on the bedpost.

'The damn bullet! … Everything's going dark … so dark … Jens … I'm dying! … I – I'm dying!! … Ida! Mother! … They were so proud of me … Ah! Doctor? … Congratulations, my dear boy! … Congratulations! … But, I … I want to! … No, Nora! just a frog, child! … Look! … the sea … it's all turning … black … so black … Mother! … Mother … It will all be fine … fine … Ah! Aaah!! … Good night … h! – h! – Good night, Doc … D- … Doc – Doctor …'

'Leave off a little! – He's calming down!'

Jens straightened up. His breathing was difficult, laboured.

He looked at his wrist. It was blue. A few bloody streaks ran across it.

'Put out … the … lamp! It's carbonising!'

Olaf sank back into his armchair, exhausted.

Now the room was getting brighter. The brass doors on the white tiled stove by the door gleamed faintly. Outside the sparrows began to chirp. There was a horn blast from the port.

The courtyard door had opened below. Someone was shuffling across the yard. A bucket was hooked to the pump. Now the pump handle squeaked. The water rushed into the bucket in spurts. The figure went back slowly across the courtyard. The door was closed again.

They looked at the bright window. Involuntarily they both exhaled deeply.


'Hey! Olaf! Look!'

Olaf didn't answer. He had merely turned his head a little towards the bed.

'He's lying there like he's dead!'

'I think ... Hmmm!'

He checked his watch.

'We have to put on a new bandage! Give me the ice pack!'

Jens handed him the fresh ice pack from the table. They carefully changed Martin's bandage.

Olaf mumbled something incomprehensible into his long, straw yellow moustache.

'I think the wound was – not cleaned carefully enough! I'm sure there are still bits of fabric from his trousers in there! ... Look!'

They had both bent down over the gunshot wound on the side of Martin's abdomen.

'Hey! Just look! ... He's really changing!'

'Hmmm!'

'He's lying so still!'

'Yes! We have to send for the doctor!'

'Shall I ring the bell?'

'Yes!'

Jens hurried to the door. The bell rang loudly through the quiet building …

The first ray of sunshine now flashed golden over the roofs into the room. It spread its bright glow on the dark blue wallpaper above the bed and traced the window crossbars against the wall at an angle. The spines of the books on the shelf gleamed, the glasses and bottles on the table began to sparkle. The arabesques of the shiny bronze frame around the small photograph glittered on the table amid the white, torn bandages and the dishes. The sparrows made a crazed din on the roofs outside. A few women were talking loudly in the courtyard below.

'Good God! Truly a squalid household here!'

Jens, who was walking to the sofa, had tripped over a pair of boots that were lying on the skewed, dusty carpet in the middle of the room.

'My head feels completely numb!'

He had sunk heavily back onto the creaking sofa. Olaf had not responded.

Jens stretched.

'By the way … it was a dashing duel!'

'Yes! Most proper!'

'Yes! Most honourable! – For both of them!'

'Eversen has gone abroad, hasn't he?'

'Probably!'

Jens looked thoughtfully at the two gleaming

pistol barrels above the sofa. –

'What if they come now?'

'Hmmm!'

'Ach!'

Jens yawned nervously.

'Where can that old – earwig be?!'

'When can they get here?'

Olaf had raised himself from the bed.

'After six, I think?'

'Hmmm!'


… 'Finally!'

Jens had jumped up. He hastily unlocked the door.

'Good morning, gentlemen!'

'Good morning, Frau Brömme!'

Small and scrawny, Frau Brömme stood in the doorway with her taut, worried, wrinkled face. Her small, grey eyes were fixed on the bed, half questioning, half disgruntled. She tugged at the string of her apron with her thin fingers.

'How is he, sir?'

'Bad! You should send for the doctor as quickly as possible!'

Olaf had not looked up from the bed.

'Oh dear God! … But it will …'

'And … bring some fresh water, please!'

'Yes! Right away! Right away! O dear God! Oh my God!'

These last words had already come from out in the corridor.

The room next door was now coming to life. A window was opened. Someone tuned a violin.

'The philologist! He gets up at six every morning and plays! Couldn't we open the window a little? It's suffocating in here!'

'Yes! A little!'

Jens opened it. Taking a deep breath, he inhaled the fresh morning air.

The philologist was now playing the violin next door, the strains of an old folk ballad resounding softly, plaintively around the sunny courtyard amid the chirping of the sparrows and the cooing and the flapping of the pigeons. From a distance, through the clear morning air, the bright trembling toll of a church clock.

They both listened. Their pale, exhausted faces were most grave … There was now a rattling at the door. Jens opened it. Frau Brömme entered with the bucket of water and coffee. She scuttled carefully towards the table. She kept her eyes on the bed the whole time.

'Here … here, sir! Some coffee, gentlemen! Dear God, yes!'

Olaf dipped a towel in the bucket and wrung it out. It splashed. Frau Brömme nodded.

Jens sipped his coffee.

'Look at the poor young man! Oh my God! You know, that duelling, it truly is a sin!'

'Er – so is the doctor coming soon?'

'Right away! Right away, sir! Right away! Oh God! Such a young man, his mother pinned all her hopes on him! I'm sorry! But you have to admit, gentlemen!

And all for a trifle, for nothing, if you see it that way. It's true, gentlemen!'

Olaf and Jens had adopted highly reserved expressions.

'Oh yes! You can live through a thing or two when you rent to students for twenty years!'

Tired, Olaf had sank back in his chair.

'Oh, you must be good and tired too, sir! … Yes, you could write a book about it! Wouldn't you say? There was a Herr Eriksen who once lived next door, and he went completely delirious! Here! In my house! Oh God, if I could only …'

'Hmmm! … Could you – bring up some more ice!'

'Ice! Ice! Yes, yes, sir! Right away! Oh dear God!'

She scuttled out.


'Old witch!'

Olaf had hissed this between his teeth. Jens shook. He was shivering with cold.

'Ghastly!'

The ballad next door could still be heard through the thin wooden wall. The flies began to hum in the room …

'Hey!'

'What?!'

'He's lying unusually still?'

'Yes! … And … God! Look!! His nose is – so pointy? And … his – eyes …'

Olaf had quickly bent over Martin.

There was a cramped smile around his mouth now. His arms lay stretched over the rumpled bed. His sharp, pointed face, on which the sun now fell at an angle, was as pale as wax.

'There's … there's no – pulse at all – any more …'

'What??'

'Oh … he … so he's dead??!'

'W …??'

'Dead!!'

'Dead?? … You mean … dead???'

The words remained stuck in Jens's throat. He was trembling.

'Dead?'

It was as though he were chewing on the word.

'It … it … I will … the landlady …'

'Don't!'

Olaf had bent low over the corpse. He closed the eyes …

A minute had passed. They hadn't dared look at each other.

Now there were light steps coming up the stairs.

The landlady was talking to someone.

They looked at each other.

'Someone's coming!'

'Oh … probably – the doctor!'

Jens tugged at the bottom button of his jacket. His breath wheezed softly. They looked intently at the door.

Now …

'C- … come in'

'After you, ladies! Oh dear God! … After you!'

They had now shrunk back from the bed. They hardly dared look up.

In the open door stood a slender, elderly lady in a simple black tunic dress. Still half in the hallway was a fresh, pretty little face anxiously peering over her shoulder as though searching for something.

Quietly, with a half smile, she had now stepped into the muffled, forbidding room. She had raised her gently trembling hand, with a narrow gold band glittering through a purple twine glove, as though posing a question …

Now she had leaned over the corpse …

Outside the sparrows twittered, the pigeons cooed in the dazzling morning sun. A bright bar of teeming sun dust stretched from the window to the bed. The gentle strains of the violin were still coming from next door.

'Mama!!!'

# 'TRANSLATOR'S INTRODUCTION' TO PAPA HAMLET

In light of the interest in young, powerful, emerging Norwegian literature which has been in evidence for about a decade in almost all western countries, and which has been boosted in recent times by Ibsen's successes in particular, I considered it a not unworthy task to finally allow my German compatriots access to an author whose works, while currently far from receiving their due even in their Norwegian homeland, are nonetheless sure to attract general attention in the near future.

The author is Bjarne Peter Holmsen.

Born on 19 December 1860, the third son of a strictly orthodox country pastor in Hedemarken, he spent his childhood in the old trading city of Bergen. One of his uncles, his mother's brother who worked as a lawyer there, took him in to relieve his parents, whose offspring had further increased in the meantime.

But young Bjarne's progress in grammar school was most mediocre. He gave his uncle little joy. There were no apparent indications that he might ever succeed him. And, in fact, he did not. Whether this was due only to his minimal talent for the humanities is an open question. In any case, the fact is that the future author of *Papa Hamlet*, with its splendid humour which will surely sate the readers of this book, failed hopelessly in Christiania after only his first exam. Much of the blame for this may lie with a volume of poems whose title of *Mayflies* was indicative of the young poet's mood at the time. A fact that we may judge of equal psychological importance is that the young poet wrote by far the greatest number of these 'mayflies', to which no great originality might be ascribed, in the dissection theatre of an anatomy department. So his later predilection for the bare reality of things was still quite split at the time. It was only the discovery that his 'mayflies' really had been what he prophetically issued them as, namely mayflies, their pitiable existence soon coming to an abrupt end on the scrapheap, that appears to have tipped the balance.

He couldn't seem to make anything of his studies. His uncle's renewed attempt to keep him in academia by persuading him to enrol at least one term in the theological faculty failed. With this Bjarne Peter Holmsen's academic career came to an end. He was lost forever …

His father, who had seen his hopes sorely dashed, was reluctant to give his consent for his son to become a merchant. It was only when his uncle who, himself childless, and despite the many worries his nephew had caused him favourably disposed to him, expressed his willingness to send him abroad for this purpose, that he succeeded in overcoming his concerns.

The glorious life out in the world, the new impressions, the daily routine of work and, evidently no less important, the years spent away from home – this is what they were counting on. And indeed, this time they had not miscalculated. Once young Bjarne returned to Bergen after three years of taxing work in a London banking house, which was followed by a further two-year stay in Brest, his family had good reason to be satisfied with him.

The only blow to this satisfaction came when they finally discovered that the young banker had been playing at writing on the side. Like most of his compatriots who owe their development to time abroad, he too had returned with ideas and views that were not entirely suited to the confined circumstances of his homeland. So what more natural outcome could there be than that the old poet in him should now revivify; especially as the great new literary accomplishments of his people, the significance of which he only now fully comprehended, could not fail to influence him as well.

Admittedly, one might state that this influence was not unlimited.

From the pieces presented here, which I was inspired to collect not least because of their undeniable originality, the reader may already apprehend how rapidly our poet succeeded in his struggle to attain his own individual voice. In fact I would aver that his means of portrayal and his unflinching energy, models for which one may search in vain even among his native Norwegian literature, contain seeds which, once fully developed, will flourish far beyond the boundaries of convention. One senses it to be the vibrant product of a time of which it is said that its anatomists are poets and its poets anatomists. –

The translation was, as the foregoing suggests, exceptionally difficult. The specifically Norwegian expressions with which the original predictably swarms had to be scrupulously avoided in the German rendering. But I believe I have succeeded in this in most cases. I have spared no effort in replacing them with local alternatives wherever I could.

It is not my place to offer a critique of my author here. But I readily confess that in my studies of him he became more dear to me the more closely I engaged with him. I should be pleased if the readers were to feel the same.

It should surprise no one that the basic colouring of almost all of his works, which the young writer significantly enough refers to as 'studies' rather than finished works of art, is a gloomy one. It is the midnight sun of his Nordic homeland that casts its wan light over them. In part, of course, they may also bear the influence of circumstances of a purely personal nature. A persistent malady of the eye forced him, barely twenty five years old, to renounce his practical work. And we can only assume that the writer in him now feels impaired by this condition too.

His splendid social novel *Fremud*, which he is currently preparing for publication, will reveal whether this condition is threatening enough to arouse more serious fears for this capacity.

In any case, this would be yet another reason to

champion the writer's cause. May he avoid the fate of his great compatriot Bjørnson, whose best novella had already circulated in more than 70,000 copies in the original before it was finally translated into German, a full 20 years after it was first published.

# NEW FOREWORD TO
## PAPA HAMLET

The foreword to the first edition of *The Selicke Family* offered the best account at the time on the genesis of *Papa Hamlet*. But as this has now been replaced by a new foreword to mark the third edition, it appears not undesirable for us now to reprint it on the occasion of this collective edition of our writings.

It read:

In January 1889, exactly a year ago now, the *Carl Reissner* publishing house in Leipzig issued a new publication to the book market entitled *Papa Hamlet*, the author of which was stated to be a hitherto entirely unknown Norwegian by the name of *Bjarne P. Holmsen*, while its translator was named as Dr *Bruno Franzius*. This book was a mystification, and the undersigned were its authors.

What was their motivation? It was the old, oft-heard complaint that only foreigners receive appreciation in this country, such that to take certain risks with impunity one must be at least French, Russian or Norwegian.

As a German, one would be consigned to old patterns from the outset, it was only others who were permitted to fearlessly cast off old prejudices, only they could strive for those 'new goals'! In other words: Quod licet Jovi, non licet bovi!

We were of the opinion that this complaint was based purely on a misinterpretation of the facts. We believed that the familiar, dismissive attitude with which our compatriot critics address us young people has absolutely nothing to do with our Germanness; that it is in fact completely indifferent to it, and that it is only concerned with our 'movement' *per se*! We firmly believed that we would be overwhelmed with the usual compliments, even if, for example, we presented ourselves as Norwegians! We were in no doubt that the struggle that rages today is no longer that between domesticity and foreignness, but merely – please forgive our malleable expressions – between idealism and realism, between convention and natural will! And indeed our experiment has confirmed our hypothesis …

This mystification worked splendidly. As utterly transparent as it was, and as easy as it may now be for some to claim retrospectively that they had seen through it from the outset, people believed in the existence of Bjarne P. Holmsen for a full seven months and only discovered his *non*-existence after the authors ceased to conceal it.

One of the first 'revelations' was an article by *Kaberlin* in the first November issue of the *Magazine for Domestic and Foreign Literature*.

It began:

'The author of the drama *Before Sunrise, Gerhart Hauptmann,* happily acknowledged a certain *Bjarne P. Holmsen* on the first page of his book. It was that man's novella cycle *Papa Hamlet,* published by C. Reissner in Leipzig, which, as the dedication states, had provided the decisive impetus. Once again, I thought, taking the book in hand, pollination has come from abroad; so it seems that German Realism is still not ripe for independence – rather it is compelled to substitute servitude to the French with servitude to the Nordics.

However, once I had read the first of the three novellas, the authenticity of the local Norwegian colouring already seemed highly dubious. Because all too soon it is interrupted by that natural, warm element of humour that is common only to the Germanic tribes of the central zones. And research confirmed my suspicion: it turned out that behind the name Holmsen is a young German writer who is already known as a pioneer in the hitherto rather obscure area of German Realism: *Arno Holz,* the author of the *Book of Time.*'

Two issues later the same organ then published the following letter in response to this essay. We herewith reprint it to prevent any such interpretations of our cooperation in the future once and for all.

Dear Sir!

Please allow me to make the following cordial correction to the essay 'Neo-Realistic Novellas. Discussed by Kaberlin' in number 45 of your journal:

After the author of the article in question – which incidentally is the most detailed and dignified article of those that have thus far addressed *Papa Hamlet*, at least in the German press – named me as the author of this book, he added in the form of a small footnote:

'*Johannes Schlaf* is also said to be involved in the work, but only to a secondary degree.'

Well! He is not only said to be, he is! And as far as our, that is, his and my knowledge of the situation extends, it is moreover entirely unjust to assign a 'first' or 'second' degree to either of us, regardless of which. On the contrary! Not only do we fancy ourselves to have conducted our work in equal measure, we actually did so!

A friendship of long standing, intensified by an almost equally long, close cohabitation, and certainly no less influenced by certain similarities in our natural dispositions, has gradually made our individualities, at least in purely artistic relations, almost congruent! In this context we can barely think of an issue, no matter how trivial, in which we diverge. Our methods of capturing and of reproducing what has been captured have completely converged over time. There are passages, even entire pages, in *Papa Hamlet* for which we are absolutely incapable of determining whether the original idea belongs to one, and the subsequent form to the other, or vice versa. Often the same words of the same sentence flowed into our pens at the same time, often one of us completed the sentence that the other had just commenced. So perhaps we might say that we 'told' the book to each other; we imagined it for each other, with increasing clarity until it was finally on paper. We would be no more willing to retrospectively declare that this passage is the work of one and that one the work of the other than we would be capable of actually determining it. We haven't the slightest interest in doing so! Even now, our joy that it should exist and the work itself strikes us as more important than the workers. We are already penning another, more extensive opus, and it remains to be seen whether or not it will confirm what we assume to be the 'unity of our two natures'.

With the assurance of my greatest respect,

*Berlin,* 1 November 1889.
Your most devoted *Arno Holz.*

# THE PAPER PASSION

A small Berlin kitchen, up four flights of stairs, around Christmas time. It is almost dark. Only the range fire trembling above the lid, with a few sparks from the ash chute spattering into the coal bin now and then.

Mother Abendroth is sitting there with a large brown earthenware pot between her knees, grating potatoes. Her fat, round face is bathed scarlet red in the reflected glow of the stove before her, her hair black and smoothly parted. She is wearing a dark brown woollen bodice fastened with a colourful brooch bearing a portrait of Queen Louise.

The clock is ticking above the bed, intermittent gusts of wind cast snow against the small window. Meanwhile there is an occasional low rattling of window panes amid the muffled clatter of the factory in a rear block beyond the courtyard.

'Oh God yes! – Yes I say! That wench!'

The grater has slipped into the mash, she taps it against the rim of the bowl.

'I tell you! It's killing me! My whole body! It's giving me consumption! That wench!'

The small silver rings in her earlobes tremble, and again there is a rhythmic scratching in the kitchen.

'No! No! That wench! That … pfff! Oooh awful!! I tell you! Why not come straight out with it? That bitch!! Well come on then! I'll tell you a thing or two! What?? … One … and two …'

The clock above bed has begun to strike, Mother Abendroth counts.

'… and four … and five … What, six?! Well, this is a fine day! Well knock me down! That bitch!'

'The biggest wallet,
The biggest wallet,
Belongs to Ladewich, Ladewich,
The biggest wallet …'

Mother Abendroth is listening attentively!

Outside a high, slightly hoarse voice; slowly it comes trudging and singing up the stairs.

'The biggest wallet …'

Now the front door opens.

'Belongs to Ladewich, Lade …
Oh, what!! —
Hibbledy dibbledy dippety dappety,
Zebbedee bebbedee colour and clappety,
Zebbedee bebbedee buff!'

Now, finally, the kitchen door opens.

'Evening Mother!'

'Mmm!'

Surprised, Wally stands in the doorway. She is a little, blond, scrawny thing, eleven years old. She tries to wipe away the snowball from the front of her jacket as quickly as possible, she stutters.

'I … I …'

'Mmm!'

From four storeys below in the cellar tavern comes the thin sound of an accordion, now quite clear: 'Look now, there he goes, tripping lightly on his toes' … Mother Abendroth positions herself in the middle of the dark kitchen, hands by her sides … 'Look now, one and all, here's the drunken son-in-law …'

'Eee! – Look! – So you did?!'

'I … I have … Liese!!'

'What?? Liese?? – Oh yes, you tramp! Have – I – not – told you that you need to be back by four?! Huh?! And now it's six!!! Just you wait! I'll show you! Bitch! Lord, disgraceful!! And it's the third time now!! You've been running round with those damn urchins again! At the Christmas market! Tramp!!!'

'Oh, Mama?! Mama?! I want – to – Mother!! Mother!!'

'Take that! – And that! – Ugh! – Ugh! – I'll show you!! … I'll tan your hide!'

'Mooooother! – Mooooother!!'

'I'm up to my neck with the consumption because of you! … Rude, mangy tart, you!!'

'Mo … ther!! – Mo … ther!!'

'Will you be quiet?! – Are you going to be quiet?! … Well?! Clucking around like an old turkey! I'll show you! Always running around!

Huh?! School work and all that – oh that's nothing! Nothing! God, well! I tell you! What will become of the girl? – – Just you wait!! Do you really think I'll let you become some bitch who runs around with the fellas?! Huh?! – I'd sooner break every bone in your body!! I'd sooner string you up!!!'

She now shuffles over to the kitchen table, raises the lamp with a single movement, angrily shaking the old thing back and forth.

'There! Here! And there's no oil left either! It wouldn't bother you if I sat around here in the dark! Huh?! – You've got nothing but rubbish in your head!! But you never think about anything!! You old dozy dope!! … Oh, what now? Come on! Huh?! – Are you going to get up now?! You can take another little wander!! – Now you're getting petroleum, understand?! – Well? Hurry up?! – I'll get you moving!! Slowcoach! – There! Here! Hold your hand out!! – Well? And the bottle? Of course! Nothing again!! Hold on – tight, you stupid old lump, hold on tight! …'

At last Wally is out the door again. A few more sobs can be heard from outside, then the front door slams shut.

'Oh God, am I right! I tell you!'

Mother Abendroth sits down on her chair again and gets back to grating the potatoes. Outside, someone is shuffling lazily down the stairs. Some time goes by. The small, flashing dot dances on the zinc lid of the long pipe in the corner cupboard, a few gold threads flutter between the two blood-red tassels at the top of the mouthpiece … Another heavy, iron-laden wagon has just rattled through the gateway to the courtyard. A few workers shout and laugh, and someone must have opened the windows down in the cellar tavern; the accordion has fallen silent, and the clack of billiard balls can be clearly heard. In between, regular sounds of steam from the factory.

'Oh God, yes!' …

Finally the front door creaks and someone hastily scrubs the snow from their feet on the straw mat, to the sound of Wally laughing and chatting.

'What's that?'

Mother Abendroth listens for a moment.

'I see!'

'Ah! You've got to be joking! – Tell me: honestly!'

The kitchen door opens, the red point of a burning cigar now glows out in the small, pitch-dark hall. A cough …

'Herr Haase?! Tell me …'

'Well?! Come in then!'

'Evening, Frau Abendroth!'

The round, red point outside rocks up and down quickly a few times, then a door opens somewhere in the dark.

'Ah! Evening! Well?! Come a little closer, Herr Haase!'

'Oh, if … hmmm … if you don't mind?'

'Oh, what! Why would I?! Come on in!'

'Evening! … 'Evening!'

'Evening to you!'

Herr Haase enters shyly. A tall, narrow-shouldered individual; he has a thick, patent leather college portfolio clamped under his arm.

'Mother! Herr Haase says …'

'Well?! Put the bottle down first, huh?! Dozy bitch!'

Wally slumps for a moment, but then looks Herr Haase right in the face again.

'Oh, Mother! Look how red Herr Haase's nose is!'

'Well?! You watch it! This just keeps getting better! Will you wait until you're asked, snot-nose?!'

Herr Haase now buries his big, red, crooked bird's nose in his handkerchief. He blows his nose.

'Hmmm! – Terrible weather today!'

He presses even closer to the stove, his thin voice trembling with the cold. Mother Abendroth is busy with the lamp.

'Oh yes! It's coming down out there!'

'Hmmm! – What I …'

Herr Haase absent-mindedly looks at the damp, chewed end of his cigar stub. Wally has climbed into the chair by the window and is now trying to see through the frozen panes to the courtyard below.

'… What I … wanted to say, Frau Abendroth. I …'

His portfolio slips onto the floorboards, he bends down after it. Slowly the oil gurgles in the lamp.

'… I – wanted to ask you, Frau Abendroth, if you might – just have a little – patience for a few days, by which I mean to say … with the rent! I …'

There is no answer from Mother Abendroth; Herr Haase now wipes his sleeve over the folder several times.

'… I – you know, I …'

Meanwhile Mother Abendroth has screwed her lamp back together and is now blowing into the burner.

'Pff! – Oh, don't worry about it, Herr Haase! Pff! … Pff! … that – Pff! – that isn't worth worrying about!'

The lamp now casts its light through the kitchen. Wally, who has been listening attentively, quickly turns back to her window as if caught out. She has stuffed her pinafore into her mouth, her bony shoulders shaking with suppressed giggles. Herr Haase is now even more stunned, Mother Abendroth turns around to look at her in disgust.

'Well? What's the matter, old goose?! You want the back of my hand again, huh?!'

'Hmmm! – You … You know how it is! – My – mother always gets her rent so late … and …'

Herr Haase nervously turns his stub in his fingers.

'… and – I probably shan't be able to give you the whole amount this time, either!'

Mother Abendroth puts the lamp on the table; she doesn't say a word.

'It's just that I've … I've lost a pupil now … and … hmmm!'

There is a snort from the window.

'Hmmm! – Well! – I'll go across now!'

Herr Haase has already put his hand on the door handle.

'But … what for?! – Why don't you stay here for a bit! You'll be just as chilly over there!'

'But … I …'

'Oh, stay, why don't you! – Wait! – I think – I still have … will you have a cup of coffee, then?'

'Oh … That is – most kind!'

Herr Haase shyly leans against the stove again, in the corner there's a snuffling, like someone choking. Herr Haase involuntarily looks down at his very short trousers.

'Well?! … Well? Come on! – Yes?!'

Herr Haase is blowing his nose again.

'… Well! I tell you! – That brat! – The trouble I've had? – Ach, let me tell you!'

Mother Abendroth now lifts the small, soot-blackened blue saucepan from the glowing stove ring; the red flame flares up through the small, circular opening in the middle.

'Yes! – About the rent, you know … I really could do with it, but … Ach! Dammit! All burnt again! I tell you!!'

Mother Abendroth grumpily pulls the hot rings over the fire hole again.

'Oh! Only until the fifteenth! If you could just be patient until the fifteenth …'

'Yes! Yes … See! – It's just that …'

She pours the hot, steaming coffee into a large blue marbled cup and slowly mixes a few spoonfuls of cooking sugar into it.

'… I mean! – Look! I get thirty marks from my Karl at the moment. Well! And then I have the rent from Herr Röder and the Fräulein there in the front room. You see! And I'm supposed to live on that and pay the high rent! – And you wouldn't believe how expensive everything is now! For that little bit of butter I have to pay seventy pfennigs …'

'Seventy …'

'… seventy pfennigs in the market hall! Yes!

You wouldn't believe it! – Well! But let's forget about it! If it's not there, it's not there!'

She presents Herr Haase with the steaming cup.

'There! Drink up now!'

'Hmmm! – Thank you! Thank you very much!'

Herr Haase has turned a little red again. He picks the cup up carefully. It is full to the rim. He sips in small, satisfied gulps.

'Oh God yes! I tell you … this life!'

Mother Abendroth sits down on her chair again and puts the bowl on her lap.

'And this swill! What? – But when it's this cold it does you good!'

'Oh! Not at all, it's – excellent!'

Herr Haase breathes deeply, he is smiling now. Mother Abendroth puts her arm over the edge of the bowl and blinks at him good-naturedly.

'Well, just you wait! Once you're a professor!'

Herr Haase quickly bends over the cup again.

'But – you will have long forgotten old Abendroth by then, huh?'

'Oh!'

Mother Abendroth laughs.

'Ah! Then you'll be rolling in it! Right, Herr Haase?'

The empty cup that Herr Haase places on the stove rattles.

'You??! – I'm telling you! – Don't go running your unwashed mouth off at everything!'

'Oh God! – Don't worry about it! – Where's the harm?'

'Well! What?! It's true! Really! You wouldn't believe what I have to put up with from the brat! – One moment I've beaten her half to death; the next it's like nothing happened! – I tell you, she's hard that bitch, hard as a dog! – Well, I'm just saying! With this girl! – God! I tell you! Such a great big twelve-year-old brat! Nah! – At least she had a bit of respect for my Fritz, while he was still alive! But me? – God!'

She has dropped the grater and is now looking reverently at the broken rosette above the wardrobe.

'Oh … Why did the good Lord not leave me my little Marie!'

Herr Haase coughs slightly. He looks at his cigar stub a little uneasily.

'That was a child! – God! I tell you! – You should have seen her eyes! – Well! – I … when … in a word … you see! That a child like that has to die and I have to worry myself sick over this rude mangy madam! No! … I … God! – I tell you! … No!'

She can no longer speak. The clock ticks, the fire crackles. The thin, monotonous peal from the Sophienkirche steeple can now be heard from the street. It's the evening service. In between, from the bel étage below, a piano. A lady sings. Now and then she stops, always at the same point. From the asphalted gateway the muffled clatter of horses' hooves again and the clanging and clattering of iron bars. —

'I can still see her! She was already on the way out! – You see! And it was her comforting me!

– Weep not, Mother, she said – Oh you wouldn't believe the way she could talk! – Weep not, Mother dearest! All is well with me! I am going to the Heavenly Father now! And we shall all see each other again!'

Mother Abendroth says this slowly, distinctly, as though she were reading from a hymnal.

'What do you think of that! A twelve-year-old child with a mind like that! – Sometimes I think – was it really right of our Lord to take the little grub from me? … No, you know! It eats me right up! It eats me right up!!!'

She taps her thick, broad chest several times with her round fist, Herr Haase steams and stares straight ahead with his eyes wide open.

'But d'you know what? That child could still be alive today, I tell you! – I put her in the welfare hospital back then, see! And they throttled my poor girl! – I didn't really have the money, you see! She didn't have the right care, I tell you! – Oh, I remember! Sister Anna, what a bitch she was! Acting all innocent in front of you, you know! But she was a sly old one! Well, I could tell you a thing or two! … I would have been happy to keep the poor child here; but would you believe it? My Karl couldn't stand the sight of the poor grub! – Actually she wasn't even really my own child! I had taken her off my sister. That cow had eleven children out of wedlock! So my Karl says: why should we have to feed that cow's children! You see! And that's why he couldn't stand Wally either. – Well, I ask you! What can the poor, innocent little lamb do about that! But you wouldn't believe what a grumpy old rascal he was! … Well! I tell you! I would rather die – so help me God! – than live from his good graces again!'

It is silent again for a moment. Wally presses herself against the window, shaking with the cold.

The layer of white snow on the empty bottles, withered flower stalks, rags, and the scraps of meat wrapped in newspaper on the broad, green-painted windowsill outside grows thicker all the time. The fine powdery snow gathers in the corners of the window panes. The light glitters on it at an angle from the bright windows of the side block. The wind rustles in the withered, snow-covered leaves of the flower stalks …

'No! It still eats me right up! It still eats me up! …'

'Brrrng, brrrng!'

'Oh! Christ! Yes! …'

'Brrrng, brrrng!'

Mother Abendroth is listening!

'Well! Are you going to open the door?! Didn't you hear the bell you old dope?!'

Wally winces, puts her head out.

Herr Haase exhales.

'Evening, Mother Abendroth!'

A round, red head pushes its way through the crack in the door. A pair of short-sighted eyes blinking behind a pince-nez. A small blue student cap balanced on cropped, white-blond hair.

'Evening, Herr Röder! Well, you know! …'

Mother Abendroth bends forward over the bowl from her stove corner.

'You're another of my fine runabouts! Just you wait! Hasn't been home all day!'

She laughs and winks at Herr Haase.

'Oh it doesn't matter! There's a little good in everything!'

Herr Röder has forced his way into the kitchen behind Wally.

'Good evening!'

He offers Herr Haase a very low, ceremonious bow.

'Evening! Evening!'

Herr Haase teeters up and down hastily a few times, almost dropping his portfolio again.

'Earlier on I …'

Herr Röder lets his glasses drop and cleans them with his handkerchief.

'… Earlier today … I found a man for you!'

He puts his glasses back on his red, spotty snub nose and is now staring at Mother Abendroth.

'What's that?'

Mother Abendroth laughs. Herr Röder leans casually with his thick, broad hump against the door frame.

'Must be a fine young thing!'

'Well! Indeed! … But he is a bit hunchbacked!'

Wally laughs.

'Now listen here!'

Now Herr Haase is smiling politely as well. Herr Röder remains quite serious.

'He's also a little blind!'

Wally is now jumping up and down with pleasure, clapping her hands and almost choking with laughter.

'Hmmm! That's an advantage!'

Mother Abendroth smirks.

'And a bit lame too!'

'Oh yes?! It's Lazareth himself! Anything else?!'

'Otherwise a strapping seventy-year-old!'

'Well! – Too bad!'

'Eh! … But – he has dough!'

'Ah! Well off you go then! … Aah! – You … Nah …!'

Mother Abendroth laughs until she has tears in her eyes.

'Christ! – Well … I always say … you've got to have a bit of fun!'

She wipes her eyes with the back of her hand.

Herr Röder has turned ceremonious again.

'So: about supper?'

'Today we're having potato pancakes!'

'What?? – Ah! … You! – No! – Young lady! I shall never forget you for this!'

Herr Röder is in ecstasy again with his fat, round arm outstretched dramatically. He gives Mother Abendroth a look of complete devotion. He has placed his round, fleshy hand near his heart on his thick, brown winter overcoat. He sighs.

'No! … I'll scream! … I …'

Mother Abendroth leans with her back to the wall. She is gasping for air.

'Good evening?'

'Evening! Evening!'

'No! … God! I …'

Having left the kitchen, Herr Röder now unlocks the door to his room.

'Freddy, Freddy, Frederick!
Don't be such a dirty dick!
Freddy! Freddy!
Your hair grows out your head-y!'

Mother Abendroth turns, still struggling with her laughing fit, to Herr Haase.

'Now listen here!'

The front door now closes.

'Oh God no! … Well! I tell you! … What a crank! – He puts me in a spin every time I see him! … Oh God no! … Oh! … Oh the terrible things he thinks up!'

Finally the potatoes are grating through the grater again. Next door someone is whistling an operetta melody. A chair is pushed, a boot is thrown against the thin wall.

'By the way! Did you notice? In the night he had some tart in there with him! … Well?! What are you staring at! Huh?!'

Wally quickly turns back to the window. She has been listening very attentively.

'Yes, you know …'

Mother Abendroth is whispering now.

'I've been wanting to get a laugh out of him for ages now! But do you think I can get one over on him? No way! When he comes here with his old nonsense I almost kill myself laughing! … Well, God! I say: After all, everyone has their faults! And you know, I prefer to turn a blind eye! That's just how young people are!'

'Brrrng, brrrng! … brrrng, brrrng!'

There is a ringing at the door again. Wally scurries to the hall. Mother Abendroth is listening.

'What now?! It's like the city gates in here today!'

Outside, a staid bass voice. All the while, Wally laughs and shouts.

'Well! So I'll be …'

Herr Haase already has his hand on the door handle.

'Where are you going? Stay a bit, Herr Haase! Stay a bit!'

'Oh! I … I'm in your way!'

'Rubbish! Can't you hear that? Is that Old Kopelke?'

'Hmmm!'

Herr Haase leans slowly, hesitantly, against the stove again.

'Aah! Old Kopelke! Old Kopelke!'

'Brrr! People, no … this rotten weather? You can hardly see in front of you!'

Old Kopelke limps in. He shakes his broad shoulders. He sends a cloud of powdery snow from his wide, field-grey overcoat all over the kitchen.

'Evening!'

Wally is still hanging on his arm; he is dragging her into the kitchen.

'Old Kopelke! Old Kopelke!'

'Oh yes?! … Still alive, yes?! … Evening, old

chatterbox! Well?! How goes it?'

'Ach, Mother, how do you think! You know! Such a wretched existence! You do what you can! … Evening to you too!'

He holds out his hand to Mother Abendroth. His small, watery blue, good-natured eyes twinkle, he smiles all over his smooth shaven face.

'A very good evening to you, my dear young man! A pleasure to see you!'

'Evening, Herr Kopelke! Evening! … Hmmm!'

Herr Haase smiles sheepishly and tries to get his hand free. Finally Old Kopelke lets go and turns around sharply on the heel of his boot. He tears off his woollen scarf and throws it over the bed, against which he has leaned a small, polished brown box. He moves his chair over to the kitchen table.

'Lord – take me now! … Ach! It's that damn rheumy-tamism!'

He sits down slowly, keeping his back stiff. Whenever he turns his head back and forth, a small golden pin in his right ear flickers through his hair.

'Hmmm! … Well! … And how goes it otherwise, Mother? I have to come and see for myself?'

He takes a deep breath and rubs his hands contentedly. His small eyes blink happily as he looks around the table.

'Ach, God! How should it be going? … Like a dog! On two legs! – Well, what's Mother to do? … Stay, why don't you, Herr Haase! I have plenty of room!'

Mother Abendroth takes the dish over to the stove.

'Thank you, most obliged! The old monster is in mediocre health, as the Chinese say … But you know … Hmmm! … You! Child!'

He blinks conspiratorially over to the window corner.

Wally goes up to him, he says softly in her ear:

'Bring … bring me a few onions!'

'Oh, Mother! Hoho! … Old Kopelke wants to eat raw onions again!'

A slight frown wrinkles Old Kopelke's broad, white forehead.

'No, child! No! … You shouldn't do that! It's ill-mannered! That won't do!'

'You?! … I … you know?'

Mother Abendroth unhooks the pot from the wall and sets it on the stove.

'Take a seat on my chair, Herr Haase!'

'Oh, thank you! Thank you!'

'Here, Old Kopelke! Here! Three great big ones!'

'Very good, child! Very good!'

Old Kopelke sits very stiffly on his chair, neatly picking the skin from the onions. He is chuckling with his lips pressed together and keeps his eye on the onions – there is now a hiss in the pot on the stove. A sharp smell of frying lard goes through the kitchen. It crackles and splatters.

'You must know … my dear young sir …'

Old Kopelke now turns the onion carefully between his fingertips.

'… to understand what is in your eyes … a perhaps astonishing fact … that I am peeling raw onions … and eating them raw …'

He pushes it neatly into his mouth with his thumb and forefinger.

'… that … that I am often short of air!'

Herr Haase leans back in his chair, he coughs. He lights a new cigar and smokes intently.

'Hmmm! … You – suffer from shortness of breath?'

'Pffff?!!'

Herr Haase turns around, startled. Mother Abendroth is holding her sides with laughter.

'Oh! … Oh! … Aaah! … God! That … that's a good one!'

Herr Haase looks at his cigar in confusion.

'Oh … you … you …? …'

'No, that is not exactly what I meant, dear young man! But …'

He puts the second onion in his mouth. He gives Herr Haase a very friendly look.

'… But –'

Wally has pressed close to Old Kopelke and laid her thin arms around his broad, soft shoulders.

'Old Kopelke just has a blocked stomach every now and then!'

'But – child! … You have to … That is not polite!'

'Well it's true isn't it?'

'Oh dear God! No! …'

Mother Abendroth has still not recovered from her fit of laughter. Herr Haase is smiling too now. But it is a little forced.

There is a strong smell of onions. Old Kopelke is sitting directly opposite him. —

Old Kopelke now unbuttons his overcoat, revealing his worn velvet jacket. Mother Abendroth places a few spoonfuls of the raw potato mix from the bowl in the middle of the frying lard.

'Always a fine meal here, Mother! Huh?'

'Oh, what good is bad living! That's no use to anyone!'

She doesn't look up from the pan. She narrows her eyes and lips and bends her head back. The crackling fat spits in every direction.

Next door, Herr Röder is walking up and down with heavy steps. He is singing a student song in a loud voice. Old Kopelke rubs his stomach.

'Hmmm!'

Herr Haase shudders a little.

'Hmmm! … May – may I offer you a cigar?'

'Oh! – Heh! … Well! Don't mind if I do, dear young sir! Don't mind if I do!'

Old Kopelke pinches the tip of the cigar with his broad, blunt fingernails and leans over the lamp with it.

Herr Haase exhales deeply. Old Kopelke leans back again and now happily rubs his knees with his hands. The cigar smoke forms a thin, delicate cloud around the little lamp. It makes the light even more sombre and yellow. The fat in the pan hisses, Old Kopelke hums softly to himself. Wally repeatedly kicks against his chair leg. Below, beyond the courtyard, the machines …

'Well then?! Say something, Herr Haase! You're so quiet today?'

Herr Haase starts. He has been gazing thoughtfully at the potato pancakes.

'Oh! Me? … Why do you say that?'

'It depends on the circumstances, Mother! Depends on the circumstances! Doesn't it, dear young sir?'

Old Kopelke is now stroking his mouth.

The layer on the kitchen plate with blue imagined flowers next to Mother Abendroth grows ever higher. Golden yellow, with small, brownish bumps, the pancakes arranged with a thick layer of sugar on top. They emit a fine, bluish vapour which moves to one side. It rises from the stove and goes right over the table. The whole kitchen smells of it.

'Hmmm! … Depends on the circumstances.'

Old Kopelke repeats this mechanically. He too is now looking over at the pancakes.

Mother Abendroth is fiery red. Her black, straight parted hair is shiny. Now and then she stabs the trembling, brownish pulpy mass in the pan with a fork.

'Christ, yes! … I … I feel very sorry for you sometimes, Herr Haase! … You know! … Well, don't you think? … If someone …'

She turns the pancake over.

'Well? … Just look at him! You're starving aren't you, huh?'

Wally, who is standing there with her neck stretched watching, now pushes herself against Old Kopelke. She presses her long, pointed chin on his shoulder and doesn't stop looking at the stove.

'I mean, if you always have to work and you don't have a bit on the side, a bit of rec – Well?! Ach! … Rec-re-ation, I mean! … And I say: a young person has to have that, that's what I say!'

'Hmmm! The … Oh, that … that will change!'

Embarrassed, he pushes back his green, cracked rubber cuffs and turns quite red.

'Sometimes I say to Herr Röder: Herr Röder, I say: Take a page out of Herr Haase's book! The young man sits there all day and … Brrr! This damn fat! It spits like the Devil!'

She rubs her eyes with the corner of her apron.

'… sits … sits … I tell you, the whole … day … at home … and works and can't even treat himself to a little something now and then!'

'Hmmm!'

Herr Haase is leaning far back. He puffs. His face is completely covered in smoke, next door Herr Röder sings:

'Hildebrand and his son Hadubrand, Hadubrand!'

Old Kopelke looks thoughtfully at his cigar. Every now and then he shakes his head and coughs. Mother Abendroth continues:

'No, sometimes I can't help having a good laugh about Herr Haase when he comes up those stairs with his short trousers … I mean like this! Don't I know those legs? Don't take it the wrong way Herr Haase!'

'Oh!'

'You see, the …'

Mother Abendroth turns around, surprised. Old Kopelke has suddenly begun to cough pointedly. She looks at him. He winks at her. Herr Haase fixes his attention under the table.

Mother Abendroth, who has now understood Old Kopelke, looks at him startled for a moment. Then, reassuringly:

'By the way, about what you were saying earlier, the rent, Herr Haase, no rush with that! Don't worry about it!'

'Oh, as I said, I'll get it … soon … from my mother … The money could come at any moment!'

'Erm! Hmmm! … Yes – no! … As – as I was about to say! … It's true, young sir, it's really true! Studying these days isn't like it used to be, you know! Everywhere is full up! All full up! … Ehm! … You see …'

He taps Herr Haase on the arm with his index finger. Then he turns, a little impatiently, to Wally.

'No, child! … That hurts when you press your chin like that! You have to listen to what people say!'

Wally yawns. She sits behind him on the edge of the bed and begins to gently pluck at the handkerchief in his pocket.

'Yes, if you have a lot of money, you know, you can still get by! But, you know: it's the same in every field now, I say. Look at me for instance! … Well?! With all my talents I'm just sitting around with a fat head! … Yes, precious money, you know! For instance, I once took people to court!'

He pulls a thick, greasy notebook out of his pocket.

'See, here is one case for instance … and here! Take a look! Take it, so you know I'm telling the truth!'

Mother Abendroth, laughing:

'Well! That's something else again, you know! … You could very well starve!'

Old Kopelke laughs softly to himself.

'Yes, that's true! What I earn from it, you could put it in your eye and see none the worse! But it makes you feel free, you know, when you've helped some poor devil! It makes you feel free!'

He nods good-naturedly at Herr Haase.

'Yes, you see, that's how I am! … Thank you very much! … Did you have a read? … Well! You see!'

He stuffs the notebook back into his side pocket. It is quiet for a time, Wally has pressed against the stove again.

'Well, what are you sniffing around for again! Can you move?! Have you got have cotton wool in your ears?'

Wally yawns and creeps to the window. She presses her forehead against the window frame and hums to herself.

Beyond the low, snow-covered side block across the way the factory sends dark smoke into the winter sky, aswarm with fine powdery snow. Its numerous windows gaze yellowy-red through the flurry. The large black steel rails, belts and wheels in the bright squares move back and forth continuously. There is a snuffing and groaning in regular bursts. In between, at certain intervals, a sharp, two-note squeak …

'Yes! You know, Eddy, you're always the fool! If there wasn't a bit left over from the silhouette cutting and cobbling and tinkering, things would be pretty bad for you!'

'Yes! – You're right, Mother! … But, you know? I'm getting so hungry for one of those pancakes! … Pass me one of those things, would you?'

'Here, you old gasbag!'

'Nice! Very nice! … Something that the poorest of the poor can eat!'

Herr Haase blows the smoke away, staring into the lamp burner.

'Will you have one too, Herr Haase?'

'No! No! Thanks! I …'

'Come on! Here! … Take it man!'

'Hmmm! … Thank you! Thanks! … I – er …'

Wally has turned around again, her interested piqued.

'Goddammit! … You know what … Mother! … All finished!! That makes me want more!'

Mother Abendroth smirks.

'Well, if you like it! God, yes! In bad times you can be happy to have a little bit of bread to call your own!'

Old Kopelke looks at her with his friendly, blinking eyes for a moment, then he turns back to Herr Haase. Herr Haase has already finished his potato pancake.

'But you know, young man? That can be a fine time as well you know, the studying I mean! Especially at the small universities!'

'Oh yes! But a bit raw sometimes! Very raw in fact!'

'Raw! – raw, you say? Yes, you're not wrong there! And I can tell you a fine story about that.

I mean, if you think you'd enjoy it!'

'Oh, please do!'

'I was just a young chap back then, a lad of twenty. I could be seen in polite company back then, you understand! And I tell you, I always had luck with the girlies! With the girlies – … huh, Mother?'

'What?! Well how should I know?'

'Well, at the time you took me for a dashing lad, huh, Mother? And if Fritz hadn't got in the way? …'

'Come off it! You've got that backwards! Like I ever wanted you!'

Old Kopelke laughs to himself. He looks at Mother Abendroth with great pleasure.

'Well, we'll leave it at that, Mother! Small, but oho! … No, no, you know! She doesn't want to talk about it!'

'Now stop that you old fool!'

'Well, all right, Mother! But it was good at the time! I mean! Huh?'

Mother Abendroth laughs.

'Listen to that Herr Haase! Such an old chatterbox!'

'Hey, Mother! Sundays in the park … up the Hasenheide! …

To America it's an ocean wide!
So we'd better go to Hasenheid!

I mean, Mother! But then along came Fritz. And, well you know! With a wage of three hundred talers and a cotton vest at Christmas. An old vagabond like me can't compete with that! Then she dropped me!'

'Oh! Will you be quiet?!'

Mother Abendroth quickly offers him another pancake. They both look at each other for a moment.

'Oh! Eat something yourself, Mother!'

He takes hold of the pancake with his fingertips and eats.

'Jesus said to his apostles:

Use your fingers for the morsels!

Like this! …'

He picks up the little sugar crumbs.

'So what … what I wanted to tell you, dear young sir! Back then I was in this town, in Greifswald …'

'Oh?! That's where I studied!'

Herr Haase suddenly becomes animated.

'Well, you see! … and I cut silhouettes and cobbled whenever I could! And in a tavern there I was almost beaten up by theologians because I cut out the Suffering of Christ!'

'Oh! … What?! … The Suffering of Christ?!'

'Oh yes! Old Kopelke can cut out the Suffering of Christ, the whole Suffering of Christ! … Hey! Cut out the Suffering of Christ! Yes? Do it! Oh do it!'

Wally, most interested, hops over to Old Kopelke. She

nuzzles up close to him again and strokes the front of his soft velvet jacket.

'No, child! The young man isn't interested in that!'

'The Suffering of Christ?! Made out of paper?! Oh certainly! Very! Yes, very!'

'Oh, it's just a bit of nonsense!'

'Oh just do it Eddy!'

'Do it!'

Wally is already climbing on the chair next to the bed, rummaging eagerly through a large cardboard basket on the wall.

'Oh do it! Will you? Here! The scissors!'

'Well all right! Then give me a piece of paper!'

'Mother! Give me some writing paper!'

'Writing paper? We don't have any writing paper left!'

'Well, then an old newspaper!'

'Oh yes! We have a Lokal-Anzeiger! … Here! Now make it!'

'Hmmm! The free paper it is!'

Old Kopelke carefully blows the dust off the paper and slowly begins unfolding it.

'His Majesty the Kaiser rested … hmmm! We know! Very nice! Oh, and here? A child? Huh?! Stabbed in the toilet? … Well! Look! The things that go on in the world! – Hmmm! All right! …'

He puts the cigar to one side and pulls a quarter section from the newspaper.

'No, child! No! I can't cut like that! You have to listen to what people say!'

He tries carefully to shake Wally off.

'Good God, girl! Can't you clear your legs out of it! Huh?! No, what will become of the madam?!'

'Pst! Be good, Mother! It doesn't help when you tell her off like that, you know!'

'Oh what, it's true!'

'Maybe we could clear away a bit of the chaos here!'

Old Kopelke neatly folds the paper, Mother Abendroth puts the things on the table to one side. Wally sits on the bed and dangles her legs.

'Good God, girl! Do you have to fidget with your legs?!'

Old Kopelke pinches the paper into a tiny cone that almost disappears under his short, thick fingers, and then cuts right through it.

'There!'

He licks his index finger and leafs together numerous small paper offcuts on the faded yellow tabletop.

'Well? Are we missing a little corner? … Ah here! Hmmm! … All right, and now watch!'

In the middle of the cleared space on the tabletop he places a large piece of paper that looks like a cross. Now he coughs and clears his throat dramatically a few times:

'Observe, ladies and gentlemen! This is the Cross of our Lord Jesus Christ! The Cross on which He hung, where they offered Him a sponge dipped in vinegar.'

'Hoho! Mother! That's meant to be the Lord Christ! Look! There isn't even a Lord Christ on it yet!'

Wally giggles.

'This here …'

Old Kopelke cuts out two more shreds and places them against each other with their points under the Cross.

'This here is Golgatha, known as Calvary! As you know!'

Mother Abendroth watches over his shoulders. She curls up a pancake and is chewing contentedly.

'And this here …'

'Hey, Mother!! … Listen to that – row down there!'

Everyone looks up and listens.

Heavy, dull blows from the courtyard. Between each, a shrill woman's voice.

'Heeeelp! Heeeelp! – He's – beating – me – to – death!! Heeeeelp! – Heeeeelp!!!!'

'It's the damned locksmith again!'

Mother Abendroth and Wally are already at the window. Herr Haase also leaps up. He is shaking all over.

'Heeeeelp!'

'… What's that?!'

Old Kopelke gets up as well. Outside windows warped with frost are being thrown open, a few women are calling down into the courtyard, there is already a confused frenzy of buzzing and shouting down below.

'He's locked it!!'

'Beat the door down!'

'Beat the cur to death!'

'Heeeeelp! … Heeeeelp!'

Finally Mother Abendroth manages to get the window open.

The ice-cold air whistles into the warm, steamy kitchen. The blows down below are now clearly audible. The women scream, a thick knot of people has gathered in front of a ground-floor apartment. The whole courtyard is in uproar.

'Get the policeman!! Get the policeman!! – The drunken cur is killing that poor woman!!!'

Mother Abendroth screams. She has leaned far out the window. Wally lies across her.

'Get – the – policeman! …'

Her last words turn into a cough. She is still chewing on the last piece of pancake.

'Heeeeelp!! … Heeeeelp!!'

'Good God!! – Good God!!'

The uproar below is getting louder. People are continually running through the front door of the side block. The snowflakes swirl madly down on the black, chaotic crowd of people. The great gaslight over the factory gate casts its red, unsteady light over it all.

'August, let the dragon go!!'

'Break the window!!'

'Heeeeelp!!!'

Now the patrons are coming up from the cellar tavern. A few workers emerge from the factory beyond.

'Heeeeelp!!!'

Everywhere people are leaning out their windows. Anxiously they chatter from one floor to another.

Now: a dull thud, a loud, harsh cry of fear. A few children whimper.

Mother Abendroth leans out even further. She screams as loud as she can down into the courtyard. —

'Goddammit! That was a bad blow!'

Now Old Kopelke comes to the window as well. A sharp

gust of wind blows into the kitchen and stirs up the paper Passion on the table. Herr Haase laboriously collects the individual pieces. His hands are shaking.

'For God's – saaaaake …'

Now he is standing at the window as well.

'Open up!! – Will you open up??!!'

Blows pound against a door downstairs.

A loud groan. Meanwhile the children again. The women below scream, the machines stomp and squeak in the factory beyond. At the same time, someone is calmly playing glissandos on a tenor horn in one of the rear blocks.

Now, a terrible crash! They have broken down the door. Wild roaring. In between heavy, dull thumps again. Curious, everyone now presses at the ground floor window and into the front door.

Shouting. Howling. Cursing.

'What's going on here then??!!'

A buzzing, penetrating voice, a helmet tip sparkles in the gateway.

'The policeman!! The policeman!!'

Everyone in the yard surrounds him screaming. Some are coming back out the front door. They are reporting something. Again shouting, cursing, crying.

A woman looks out at the apartment on the ground floor.

'The bastard beat the woman black and blue!!!'

Now: loud banging and crashing. A black knot of people comes through the front door. In their midst is a man, staggering; they are dragging him out.

'Cur, damn you!!'

'The cur wants beating to death!!!'

The whole crowd presses out through the gateway in

uproar. In the middle the shiny, sparkling helmet spike. - - -

Finally the courtyard is empty again. Everything is quiet again. Only a few women standing in front of the cellar tavern and gossiping. The accordion and the billiard balls can be heard very clearly again. A few people are walking back and forth in the ground floor apartment. – One window after another shuts again. Broad, yellow streaks of light from the bright courtyard windows and the red, unsteady sheen of the large lantern on the trampled snow. The stomping, roaring and squeaking of the machines and the melodic tenor horn from the rear buildings continue …

'Oh, Mother! Close the hatch, will you! There's a draught!'

Old Kopelke shivers. He has long since returned to the table.

'In a moment! In a moment!'

Mother Abendroth leans out again. She calls down into the courtyard. She is talking to someone.

'Well, just think! Such a bastard!'

'Do you have the papers, young man?'

'Here! … Here you are, Herr … Ko – pelke …'

Herr Haase can barely speak. He is still trembling all over.

'Oh I tell you! Would you believe it?! He went at her with an axe! The blood was just streaming from the poor woman's head!'

'What do you say to that?!'

'Yes, you know! And the poor woman is pregnant again!'

'Good God! Good God no!'

'And that's the fourth time now that he's

beat her like that! He'll beat her to death one day! Just you wait!'

'Well, I say: isn't it better to just string up a cur like that?!'

'Mother!!'

'Yes, yes, all right! I'm coming! … Well! Evening, Frau Scharf!'

'Evening!'

Mother Abendroth pulls back from the window. She laboriously latches the window closed. Her face is very red from the cold.

'Well, ladies and gentlemen! Is that some kind of clientèle here in the building? … Such a bastard! The factory owner ran him out long ago because of his damn drinking, the poor woman goes out begging for him and he beats her black and blue for it!'

'All right, calm down Mother!'

Old Kopelke sets the cross in the middle of the table again; Mother Abendroth is still quite beside herself.

'Oh yes! That's right! I still have to bring Herr Röder his food!'

'There! Well, well …'

Old Kopelke watches as she goes. He laughs quietly to himself and his eyes twinkle.

'… Well, watch now, dear young sir! … So that was the Cross and this was the hill of Golgatha! These two little pieces are the two thieves! To one of them the Lord Christ says: Verily, I tell you, this very day you will be with me in Paradise!'

Wally is bored. She has returned to the window and is looking down into the courtyard. A few women are talking downstairs. Mother Abendroth's voice can be heard clearly.

'Here, these little pieces under the Cross are the soldiers, and this here is the cloak of Christ that they're gambling for. You know! Well! And these here are the dice! There!'

He has now put two tiny pieces on either side of the Cross.

'This here is Mary, His mother, and this is John the Apostle whom he loved!'

'Ha! The fire! The fire!'

Wally is pointing to the courtyard. The factory chimney looming tall and black into the dirty grey snowy sky casts a red flame fluttering high into the whirling white-grey flakes.

'This here is the stick with the vinegar sponge, from which Christ drank, you understand! And these, up here are the Apostles, who are going to Emmaus … And look, there you have it, the whole Passion cut from paper! It's a fine old trick and suitable for all the family!'

Wally has come to the table again and is leaning on Old Kopelke's shoulder. Now she blows right into the scraps, they fly apart over the whole table. A few white shreds whirl around the half-lit kitchen. Only the cross remains lying crooked on the table.

'Child! You are just too rude! You've blown apart the whole Suffering of Christ again!'

Wally laughs.

Old Kopelke pinches the Cross into a taper. He lights it over the lamp and uses it to re-light his cigar. – Herr Haase mindlessly twists the two disciples from Emmaus between his fingers.

Beyond in the factory, they are now discharging the steam. At times the groaning and stomping of the machines lightly rattles the windowpanes.

'You see, dear young man? Is that not remarkable? That you can make a toy from something like that! But you know what? They almost beat me up for it! You see! I mean! If you take it like that: what a fine old world it is after all!'

He leans back leisurely in his chair, blinking good-naturedly at Herr Haase through the cigar smoke.

'Well, child? You can hand me another of those pancakes now!'

# A GARRET IDYLL

Frau Aurora Wachtel is a widow, and as her late husband, an honest craftsman, left her a most meagre bequest, she has to get by in the unreasonably large metropolis with the rent that her three mansard rooms bring.

Frau Aurora Wachtel is a short, round woman with a most lively temperament. She is astonishingly good-natured; in fact too good-natured for a city dweller. One can move her to tears without expending much effort at all. She also has the peculiar habit of seizing any remotely appropriate occasion to tell her tenants, or whoever else she can get hold of, about her late daughter, who was a paragon of all known virtues. Certainly no one whom she has regaled on the subject, through streams of tears, with an astonishing force of eloquence, has yet dared to doubt it …

On such occasions Frau Aurora Wachtel usually adds that her grief for the deceased will kill her yet, and as most of her listeners, in view of the not inconsiderable corpulence of Frau Wachtel, consider such a fear unfounded, she then usually draws a comparison between her former intellectual and physical merits and the present decline of same …

Good Frau Wachtel has moreover the peculiar habit, also somewhat dubious in a city dweller, of 'wearing her heart on her sleeve'. Any disadvantageous consequences of this are offset by another quality: despite her acknowledged good nature, Frau Wachtel can muster incredible energy and on such occasions be 'a little straightforward'. Indeed, it even transpired that she once conveyed an 'ill-mannered' tenant from one of the above-mentioned rooms with her own hands and then down the first of the four flights of stairs that lead to her apartment … In all other respects, however, she is the most admirable, most attentive landlady in the world, and if some find the vigil that she keeps over the house from the kitchen with which she and her little foster daughter make do to be overly strict and for this reason cast doubt on Frau Wachtel's aforementioned admirable qualities, one would have cause not to set great store by it …

At the time this story takes place, the three garret rooms were occupied by the following tenants.

In a one-windowed, narrow room lived a student who enjoyed a reputation for exceptional respectability in Frau Wachtel's mind. She could not be dissuaded from this good opinion by the objections of a young painter, another tenant which, incidentally, could be explained by the fact that she presented the 'Herr Graduand' to the young artist with great frankness as an example meriting imitation, in which she believed herself to be vindicated by the young man's moral conduct, which was admittedly somewhat free …

The painter would maintain that this exemplary way of life could easily be explained by the advanced state of the gentleman's studies. What's more, he could present examples to show that 'not so very long ago' he was somewhat different. But that makes little impression on Frau Wachtel when, with the most praiseworthy patience and the most respectful emotion 'Herr Graduand' allows himself to be apprised of her late daughter's merits as often as Frau Wachtel may choose, and exhibits the most noble compassion for her grief …

The painter lives in a larger, two-windowed room. He is a young man of twenty-two, of very small stature, but he makes up for it with long hair and an equally long name, which owes its expansiveness to the addition of the young man's place of birth. His name is Müller-Königsberg. Frau Wachtel declares him to be a good-natured yet extremely frivolous individual, as he never returns home before midnight as a matter of principle, and also frequently entertains ladies. He has not yet succeeded in convincing Frau Wachtel of the importance of these visits – the ladies are models. Given that, aside from a few guileless, unfinished landscapes which have been standing on their easels for some time in this state, no other traces of his industry are to be seen, Frau Wachtel believes herself justified in her admittedly unsubstantiated doubts … Frau Wachtel has not the slightest appreciation for the 'artistic' disorder that prevails in his room. Even though, as an 'old woman' she can tolerate the absolutely classical nudity of some of the numerous studies that hang all around and are not in the least embarrassed in the presence of the decorous Frau Wachtel, she is disconsolate that this 'disgraceful clutter' should so blasphemously despoil her fine room … In addition to these studies, this 'disgraceful clutter' includes some dry palm leaves, Japanese fans and parasols, old weapons, costumes, fishing nets, stuffed birds, pallets, easels, tubes of paint both empty and full, nude photographs, sketchbooks and so on, all lying around in colourful profusion in every niche and nook of the room.

But this 'artistic' disorder reaches the greatest imaginable extent following the frequent visits of student companions and like-minded fellows of the sociable young man. It is said, by the way, that his not uninteresting facial features and the artistic negligence of his exterior afford him great popularity among the ladies.

The third, smaller room is occupied by a young actor and his wife, whose declamatory exercises often drive the 'Herr Graduand' to despair. Herr Kraft and his wife were without engagements at the time and therefore quite penniless, a condition which did not, however, significantly impair their high spirits …

This amiable couple soon became acquainted with our painter by dint of the convivial virtues that both parties shared … 'Herr Graduand' was the object of recurrent minor intrigues which, however, completely failed in their effect and did not manage in the least to wrest him from his composure.

Frau Kraft was expecting, and the child had been due for some time.

When our painter came home one morning at what was by his principles – if one might even credit him with the possession of such useful qualities – a reasonable hour, he heard cries of pain from his neighbours' room, the cause of which he learned from the reassuring blandishments of a female individual. Those cries of pain lasted for around two hours, after which time they stopped and the young artist heard a brief quivering cry …

Although the little newcomer, whom I should like to introduce to the dear reader as the hero of this tale, was actually rather redundant given the material situation of the couple as described above, he was not in the least embarrassed about leaving the blissful unconscious still life of his previous state to enter the world of consciousness. Yes, and it must be said that the cry with which the curious little customer greeted the meagre garret room that was to become the scene of his young sufferings, that the way in which he demonstrated his selfhood *ad aures* to anyone who wished to hear it, testified to no ordinary life force. This force might perhaps have filled any other individual who found himself in the equivocal position of our hero's father with pardonable concern, but at a sign from the midwife he entered the meagre little room accompanied by our Frau Wachtel with the joyful, unabashed curiosity of a child summoned to his Christmas presents … Once the midwife had neatly tied the child in swaddling clothes, he took his offspring in both arms, observed him with a face radiating joy and enquired, while he rocked the child back and forth:

'A son?'

'Yes indeed, a son, Herr Kraft!' answered the

midwife, who was readying to leave.

'Didn't I say? Didn't I say?' he turned to his wife as he blushed with pleasure all over, stretched out his arm and waved his index finger up and down like a happy child.

'Didn't I say, Helene? A boy!'

His wife called for the child in a weak voice, and he carried him over to the bed, dancing, and leant down to her with him.

'Look at that! Hey! A strapping lad! And is he not the spit of me? Hey, Frau Wachtel? Look! Judge for yourself! Just like his father! There is no question, Helene! Just like his father! There is no question, Helene! Just like his father! No doubt at all!'

At which point he was about to start dancing up and down the room with the little one in the fullness of his paternal joy, whereupon Frau Wachtel protested most vigorously on the cogent grounds that the child and the mother now had to have 'absolute' rest. The happy father could not object to this reasoning and went to his wife's bed to inquire after her condition with as much tenderness as fuss. But here, too, the prudent Frau Wachtel protested. She forced him from the bed with no great restraint, laid the new-born baby down at its mother's side and then withdrew quietly into her kitchen while Herr Kraft threw himself on his leather-covered daybed and soon fell into a mellow, joyful sleep wearing a beatific smile …

Herr Kraft had played the romantic lead to great success in various provincial theatres in southern

Germany – the more important ones, as he claimed. To the not unwarranted question as to why he had given up such unusually favourable positions, he would reply that he needed a larger arena to allow his talents to develop to the full and had therefore come to the capital. Although for the time being he was 'high and dry' – as he put it – he was sure to soon find an engagement commensurate with his talents. He had already been presented with various offers, and indeed from not unimportant theatres; but they would not have satisfied him.

Yet for the moment, he and his wife, who had an unshakable faith in her husband's talents, hardly knew what to live on. He had to rely on the somewhat equivocal kindness and self-sacrifice of his mother-in-law, and he also felt compelled to take one item after another from his wardrobe and that of his wife, a soubrette, to the pawnbroker. Nevertheless, since his wardrobe was already very meagre, he spent almost all day in the room, weighing up the laurels of future great successes and declaiming; very poorly, 'Herr Graduand' claimed; he held that the man must only have played very minor roles. Of course, one does not know the extent to which one might endorse the views of 'Herr Graduand' here …

Variety in this still life, to the extent that one had need of same, was first supplied by Herr Müller-Konigsberg. But as this young, aspiring artist spent most of the day away from home, after resolving to get out of bed in the morning toward midday, the arrival of a son was most welcome to Herr Kraft, and we shall soon see what variety this young human brought to the previously somewhat monotonous domesticity of the actor couple …

At first the good Frau Wachtel put the full glory of her good-heartedness on display. She brought the new mother childbed soup free of charge and, sitting at the bedside and propping up her good-natured moon face, lost in thought, surrendered to the memories of her late daughter which caused her to weep the bitterest tears while the new mother ate the soup, breaking off from time to time to contribute regretful or consoling interjections … Frau Wachtel exhibited the most maternal care for the little one, although a certain self-discipline was required in the face of a natural habit that the helpless condition of this age brings …

The young artist was introduced to the little one soon after the birth. When he visited his neighbours, he found them in the following situation. The mother was seated on a footstool in her nightshirt before a chair, her mouth held open over an earthen pot, inhaling the vapour that it issued. For she had long suffered from persistent hoarseness and was endeavouring to overcome it in the manner indicated. She still looked most pale and exhausted, a condition partly attributable to the fact that, given her husband's present circumstances, she lacked hearty food. Herr Kraft was seated on a patent leather daybed and was busy feeding 'his boy' from a bottle with a rubber tube.

'I'm telling you, Helene …'

Here he was interrupted by the young painter's entrance.

'Ah, Herr Müller! Look, look, my dear Herr Müller! A boy, and what a boy!'

He got up and held the little boy, who did not

appreciate the interruption of his pleasant activity and so erupted in clamorous crying, towards Herr Müller. He, who had the quirk of detesting children of this age most fiercely, made a sourly sweet face and tapped the little chap's hand several times with the very tip of his index finger, saying:

'Indeed! A most adorable lad! Congratulations! A charming chap! Hmmm! Hey! Hey! You!'

As he caressed the little man in this way, his forehead broke out in a sweat.

'Isn't he?' cried the joyful father.

'And isn't he the spit of me? Tell me yourself, dear Herr Müller!'

'Certainly!'

'You see, Helene? Everyone says so! She won't believe it!'

'So give the poor grub something to drink!' she called over in her hoarse voice without changing her position. 'He's screaming himself half to death!'

This warning was certainly justified, for if our little hero paused now it was only because his voice had given out from complete exhaustion.

'Don't say that, Helene! I have heard from the best doctors that nothing is more beneficial to children than screaming, proper screaming!'

'Oh! No …' Helene answered.

'Certainly! Helene! No doubt at all! It dilates the lungs!'

'Well, the child has to drink. We don't want him to starve!'

'He must! Absolutely, he must!' replied Herr

Kraft, as he sat down again and put the bottle into the little one's snapping mouth and carefully ensured that it did not slip out.

'Of course the child must drink, Helene! But like I told you' – he had already told her before the entrance of the young painter, who was leaning against the door with his hands in his trousers and watching rather mindlessly as the little one drank – 'like I told you, this method is completely wrong-headed!'

'But …'

'Take my word for it! It is wrong-headed! That's what *I* say! Because, I ask you: is it natural?'

'But Alfred!'

'Herr Müller!' He turned heatedly to the young man. 'Tell me, Herr Müller! Is it unnatural to feed children from bottles?'

Our little hero seized another opportunity to dilate his lungs …

'Well! …' said Herr Müller-Königsberg, who did not believe himself equipped with the necessary expertise on this issue.

'You see, Helene? Naturally! No doubt: it is unnatural! You should nurse the child yourself, Helene!'

'But how can I!'

'Oh, that's an illusion! *I*, Helene! I tell you, you are healthy! Absolutely healthy!'

'Nice and healthy! With my weak chest!'

'Well, what are the Negresses supposed to do? They have the only correct method! I have read, in recognised, authentic, renowned reports, that their childbed is nothing more than a bush! And then: where would *they* find bottles with rubber tubes?'

Herr Müller-Königsberg laughed, and Herr Kraft, believing that he had unconsciously made a joke, joined in.

'But I'm not a Negress, Alfred!'

'Don't misunderstand me!' Herr Kraft adopted a paternal, instructive tone. 'That was just an example! When you consider how well Negro children do with this method in general, you must concede that the natural method by which one nurses children oneself, is best! And *I* do not consider it beneath the dignity of a civilized person to learn from even a Negro if one benefits from it, Helene!'

Herr Müller-Königsberg, who found the air in the room – the windows were almost never opened here, for it was winter, and one had to spare the furnace – increasingly insufferable and feared for his eardrums with the continued screaming of the little one, thought it best to take his leave.

'Oh stop it, Alfred! For God's sake! The wretch is screaming himself to death! Give him something to drink! But leave him alone!' She got up and seized our little hero. 'Give me it! I'll give it to him myself!' From that point on the little one was, however, deprived of the opportunity for that salutary pulmonary exercise. But he did not let it irk him, sucking avidly at the rubber hose and then falling asleep.

'No, Helene! I maintain that it would be more beneficial for the child,' continued Herr Kraft as he paced up and down with his hands behind his back. He then tried, with as much imagination as scientific expertise, to explain to his wife the highly dangerous chemical processes that the rubber must inevitably generate in the little one's mouth, and then repeated his assertion with particular emphasis.

'All of that is correct, Alfred! But it is even better if the child gets healthy, hearty milk than for me to nurse it myself with my weak breast!'

'Well, on your head be it, Helene!'

Helene lost her patience, which was no small matter since she was most inclined to apathy by nature.

'Well, what do you expect when we don't have anything proper to eat!? Today and yesterday all we had for lunch was coffee with bread and butter! The child is supposed to get stronger from that?'

'And are you blaming me for this? Helene! *You!*…'

'Well! After all, am I to blame for our misfortune?'

'Woman!!! …'

Herr Kraft clenched his fists as he rolled his eyes in a most alarming manner and his long, splendid artist's mane stood on end, and he assumed a posture of utmost aggression, such that Helene thought it necessary to accompany the reproaches she was making against him with loud sobs, which were by all means meant to appeal to the pity of her enraged spouse … After this conversation had reached a certain tragic pitch, it took a fortunate turn for the better just before what was certain to be a most awful catastrophe. The reconciliation was concluded when Herr Kraft pressed his sobbing wife to his romantic lead's breast and called her his 'dear, dear woman'. After he employed his persuasive eloquence to once again win her over to the doubtless certainty that their position would soon be highly favourable, Helene washed the swaddling clothes, and Alfred declaimed from a highly interesting book, *Humour in Court* …

Two months passed in this fashion, during which time our little hero was every day the subject of extensive discussions between the two spouses, as they were still in their room idly waiting for the favourable turn of their fate and yet obliged to fill the intervening time with the whatever distraction they could muster … He had ample opportunity to exercise the pulmonary gymnastics mentioned above. Since the views of his parents diverged with regard to his care, because each wanted to convince the other of the excellence of his or her method, our hero became the subject of a variety of experiments which, however, had no other appreciable effect on his physical condition than giving him an upset stomach on a number of occasions. The treatment of said complaint was yet another test that our hero, who in light of all these facts is well deserving of the designation, managed to valiantly overcome.

The older he grew, the more multifaceted his father's interest in him became. One day, when our hero had once again seized the opportunity to dilate his lungs, which, incidentally, he had been doing all day, which must certainly have been advantageous for his physical development, his father declared:

'Helene! The boy has an obstinate character!'

'Oh!' she said, chewing on buttered bread between sips of coffee. She was in her nightshirt as usual, even though it was afternoon, for she thought it unnecessary to clothe herself as they didn't go out anyway and they'd no cause for embarrassment in the presence of any of their visitors. Herr Kraft was of the same opinion, pacing up and down in shirtsleeves as was his habit. A similar principle had resulted in an 'irresponsible want of hygiene' in the room. This was Frau Wachtel's expression …

'Take my word for it, Helene! He has an obstinate character!'

'Oh, he is still much too small! There is no way you can tell that yet!' ventured Helene – a rare and timid objection.

'Don't believe that, Helene! That's why he's *my* boy! He's as smart and developed as a one-year-old child. Take my word for it! Haven't you seen how cleverly he looks at me when I talk to him? Mark my word!'

'Will you be quiet!!?' he shouted at the child, who, bewildered by his papa's terrifying face, fell silent.

'Do you see? He understands me! But he's obstinate! You see, there he goes again!'

God alone knows why our hero cried. He was not yet in the fortunate position of being able to express his wishes. Was he sick? Did he want for love? Did he long for a dialogue, the kind that we may only hold with our mother in this period of life, she who is capable of comprehending our every need, every stirring of life and sentiment by virtue of her all-powerful love? … Did he miss all that? Who might peer into such a little soul? …

'As I said, he's obstinate! We must seriously think about educating him!'

'Oh, dear God! The poor grub doesn't understand

anything yet!' Helene mumbled indistinctly. As she was chewing it was difficult to understand.

'Don't you believe that! You cannot start educating early enough. There have been examples of children of four years of age who learned Latin and *my* boy will undoubtedly be able to do so as well!'

From this point on Herr Kraft made the most commendable effort to combat the traces of original sin in our hero according to the principle of: spare the rod, spoil the child! … Here, of course, the evil was not driven out, but rather heightened to such an extent that their neighbours' peace was often most grievously disturbed … whereupon 'Herr Graduand' entered into a conspiracy with Frau Wachtel and enjoined her to put an end to this paternal zeal for education, but this bore no great success and Herr Kraft stated with noble indignation that he would *never* tolerate an objection to his most sacred paternal rights and obligations …

Nevertheless, one day Helene so neglected her maternal concerns that she, entirely disregarding her high admiration for her husband and her habitual apathy, completely stemmed Alfred's 'sacred' zeal by administering him a powerful slap in the face …

This unprecedented act was followed by a performance of high tragedy. It concluded with Herr Kraft donning his coat and swearing by all that is holy, by Heaven and Earth and all that dwells within them that he would leave the 'wicked sinner', 'forever'. But as she came to her senses, deeply dismayed by such a terrible decision, and took to her knees to beg his forgiveness, he finally, finally, softened, not for her sake, but for the sake of his 'unfortunate, orphaned child' … In any case, one consequence of this scene was that the part of our hero's body that had experienced the educational intentions of Herr Kraft more than any other gradually succeeded in overcoming the traces of same …

Meanwhile, a significant day had arrived for our hero, that of his baptism. This was to be celebrated with all due formality. For this purpose, Herr Kraft had sent an invitation to the young artist, to a 'model' known to the latter and to himself and his wife, and to one of his sisters, with all three persons to stand as godparents.

All manner of extensive preparations were made for this important day.

Herr Kraft decided to hock a fur coat, the last, most precious item of his wardrobe, one which had thus far weathered every storm, and Helene succeeded in clothing herself for once and went out to make the necessary and appropriate purchases.

When the great day arrived, the guests assembled at the appointed hour. Herr Müller-Königsberg had dug out an old, once black formal suit, already somewhat worn, and, with the utmost ingenuity, refurbished it by means of restorative blackener and Chinese ink as a result of which he appeared most dignified and, after revealing this artifice in his inimitably witty way, earned the compliments of all those present … The 'model', a young, highly sociable and amiable lady, appeared in an unimpeachable ensemble.

Helene had smartened herself up in an old, black silk dress. The sister, a seamstress who was highly reserved from the outset, also appeared in appropriate attire; admittedly, her ensemble betrayed far less imagination than that of the 'model' … Our little hero, who immediately received the most tender caresses from the kindly young lady, was so utterly astonished at such unfamiliar treatment that he forgot his 'obstinacy' and stared at the kindly young creature with eyes agog, and then smiled; our little hero's slight body had been laced into white swaddling clothes, polished off with a calico cap adorned with a pink bow. Once all the preparations had been made, they made their way to church …

Thanks to the fur coat they passed the afternoon and evening in the most cheerful mood. After a light meal, they settled in with coffee and cake before a more extensive dinner followed by beer and cigars. Herr Müller was sitting on the leather sofa, next to him the kindly godmother with the little one in her arms, who was most quiet today and kept smiling at the godmother – he was so truly happy for once – who kept caressing him.

The conversation soon turned most lively. The painter employed the most delightful humour to tell of a colleague who was afflicted with the physical infirmity of a squint, on account of which he was at one point drawn into an unpleasant affair. This man was at a small gathering when he got into an argument with his neighbour. But as that unfortunate infirmity made it seem as though the insults he was directing to said neighbour were addressed instead to *his* neighbour, whom he appeared to fix with his eye, a dispute arose around him, and with this too resulting in a comparable misunderstanding, he found himself quarrelling with the entire table and finally, as luck would have it, with the innocent author of this heated argument … The young man succeeded in illustrating this interesting event most vividly through mime, transporting his listeners into a state of ebullient delight …

Thereupon Herr Kraft demonstrated to the utmost degree that he was an uncommonly handsome man on the stage, and then shared one story after another from his treasury of experience, each apt to set the personal advantages of our romantic lead in the most favourable light imaginable … The mood became less and less constrained, and when Herr Müller, who, among his many other admirable qualities had an excellent bass voice, began to sing a song, the whole company joined in, except for the sister, who judged it a favourable moment to slip away. The 'model', whose tenderness had gradually cooled, had put our hero aside and was smoking cigarettes with Helene, who was unusually exuberant on this day, and puffed the smoke toward the ceiling in delicate blue rings with coquettish grace. Herr Müller-Konigsberg found her so utterly adorable in this activity that he called her his 'dearest little lamb' and stole a kiss from her red, round lips; for this she pushed him away without, it must be said, overly discouraging him. Our married couple, who found this process most amusing, burst into hearty laughter …

The fact that the narrow room was shrouded in a thick cloud of tobacco smoke did not affect the general mood of good cheer. When the 'model' at one point expressed concern about the little one, his papa insisted that it didn't matter, that he was used to it; and that might well have been the case, as other such gatherings took place there from time to time in a similar manner whenever fortunate happenstance brought money into the house, for Herr and Frau Kraft had always been very generous … They parted rather late in the most excellent mood. The young lady, who was warbling the latest operetta melodies, let Herr Müller-Königsberg escort her home, and the two left Helene and Alfred behind with somewhat heavy heads …

Herr Kraft's zeal for education took its course and found a new extension. The 'boy' was to be taught the rudiments of language. So Alfred did not shrink from spending almost a whole day trying to teach our hero the vowel *ah*, since, as he claimed, this is the easiest to produce and that one must start from the very beginning …

All the while he addressed the little pupil in a manner that one might consider worthy of a human child in his fourth year, at least … Unfortunately, our hero's innate obstinacy determined that he made little progress and often put the patience of his paternal teacher to the gravest test.

Helene, whose fortunate temperament incidentally allowed her to most adeptly pass the greater part of the day eating, drinking and sleeping, mindful of her husband's terrible threat, lodged no particularly vigorous protest, even though what she in bolder moments referred to as her common sense was often outraged. She also hoped that in time her husband would tire of passing the hours in this way. And this did indeed occur, particularly as the material situation of this admirable couple grew ever more precarious, such that they already considered it more prudent to debate said situation, if not always in a parliamentary manner. At times they lost their sense of humour most alarmingly, and unfortunately our little hero was often affected by this fact …

Under these circumstances, the small, discerning customer found it more advantageous to withdraw from the situation all together. One day he fell ill and went into convulsions; he was in the sixth month of his life …

A doctor summoned by the deeply dismayed parents was unable to save him. The little scrawny body convulsed once more, once more he rolled his eyes and then passed away in the arms of his mother, who threw herself sobbing loudly over the little corpse, while his father, the picture of mute despair, clasped his hands before the group and stared down at them …

The little corpse looked lovely as it lay there in a snow-white pinafore. With his little mouth distorted in the throes of death, it looked as though he were smiling, as corpses do … They had set the little calico cap with the pink bow on the little boy's head. It was so benign, so peaceful …

Frau Wachtel, who wept the bitterest tears over him, had folded the little one's hands across his chest …

'Yes, yes! He laughed so young! That's not good! Those children die early!' she said. Frau Wachtel was highly superstitious.

'He was a child of great, very great disposition,' groaned the disconsolate father.

His mother said nothing, simply looked at the little corpse and wept silently …

Two days later he was placed in a tiny, meagre wooden coffin which Frau Wachtel adorned with two large wreaths, and then the couple and the artist, who had once again brought out his restored formal suit for the occasion, went with the corpse to the cemetery. - - - - - - - - - - - - - Frau Wachtel went to 'Herr Graduand' and poured her heart out to him.

'The poor little grub! Why did the good Lord bring him into the world? But it is just as well that He took him away in good time! Just as well! …'

Some time later, with the expected engagement still failing to materialise, Herr Kraft decided to model in the art academy, and Helene will most likely try sewing or some such once she has overcome her immeasurable grief. - - -

You may find it strange that the writer should have chosen a hero with such a ludicrously short life span. But why should a sketch not also boast such a sketch of a hero? … There was little of interest to report about his deeds. Perhaps his sufferings were his deeds? But even that is doubtful. This you may judge as you wish, dear reader!

# AFTERWORD

For a brief moment in the late 19th century, Norwegian writer Bjarne P. Holmsen was a celebrated import to Germany's literary scene. With a book of three novellas issued in early 1889 in the translation of Dr Bruno Franzius, he captured the imaginations of the country's more venturesome reviewers and readers. His work plotted a way forward from Realism to a far more rigorous approach to subject matter, in a fearlessly avant-garde style which made just about everything else on offer at the time seem fusty, sentimental and affected. Holmsen was a major new voice in the new movement of Naturalism.

Yet at the peak of his fame in Germany, Holmsen was oddly absent from print reviews in Norway; bookstores in his native country didn't carry his works, and even a well-read Norwegian of the time would have drawn a blank at his name.

Because Bjarne P. Holmsen didn't exist.

Before the year was over, readers discovered that the book, *Papa Hamlet*, was not a translation at all, but actually the work of German writers Arno Holz and Johannes Schlaf. The pair's collaboration, which lasted from 1888 to 1892, also produced a handful of other prose pieces, a play and – improbably – an autobiographical comic. Together and separately, Holz and Schlaf would prove highly influential for the development of German literature as the new century dawned, but the implications of their writing went even further, foretelling elements of both Modernism *and* Postmodernism.

Johannes Schlaf was born in the Saxon town of Querfurt in 1862, Arno Holz a year later in what was then Rastenburg in East Prussia (now Kętrzyn, Poland). Having corresponded for a time they both found themselves in Berlin in the mid-1880s and met face to face through an association by the name of Durch! (Through!). In their individual writing endeavours Holz and Schlaf were each looking for some form of breakthrough, so their encounter in the context of a group that was at the vanguard of the city's literary activities was highly fortuitous.

Founded in 1886, Durch! was indivisibly associated with Naturalism, a movement whose presence in Germany to that point had largely been confined to foreign books, particularly those of Émile Zola, but also writers never wholly identified as Naturalist, such as Henrik Ibsen, Leo Tolstoy and Fyodor Dostoevsky. Ibsen, in particular, inspired young people at the time in a way we may find difficult to reconcile with the present-day staple of repertory theatre, while Tolstoy enjoyed an almost cult-like following in Germany, as a prophet of reform as much as a novelist.

Moving on from Realism, which had dominated European letters for much of the second half of the 19th century, these writers were united by an engagement with the uncomfortable truths of life. They questioned the social order, documented the changing status of women and the realities of sexual relations, and exposed the dire effects of poverty and its comorbidities alcoholism, violence and despair.

But as writers in Germany took up Naturalism, they transformed it into something more ambitious again. Not only did they focus on the new conditions of society, they did so through new forms reflecting the growing dominance of natural sciences and emerging technologies. Even the term 'experimental literature', which certainly applied to a number of Naturalist works, carries this association. And while Realism was less a movement and more a style that a number of writers deployed simultaneously in isolation, the adherents of Naturalism were far more social and interconnected, lending a true dynamism to their activities. In the cafes and taverns, ideas spread from table to table while theorists issued manifestos, cartographies of untrod terrain.

The new movement was accompanied by new models for living, particularly in Berlin, which offered a vivid, unruly alternative to the familiar Prussian virtues of order, austerity and discipline. To an extent that is rarely acknowledged, Naturalism was responsible for the birth of bohemian Berlin and thus the inception of the Berlin we know today, a place of hedonism, experimentation and individual actualisation – 'practical anarchism' in the words of writer Julius Bab. Brothers Julius and Heinrich Hart were the leading critical voices of Naturalism, and their Berlin apartment was a sanctuary for a revolving cast of non-conformists.

Writers and artists formed unconventional communities in or near Berlin, reflecting a bohemian ambivalence toward the urban environment. On the one hand the city allowed them to find each other, share ideas and gain work. Yet they were also repelled by its machine-like rhythms, unreflective materialism and petty bourgeois metropolitan values. The solution was some-times a half-way house – literally; somewhere between the city and the provinces many bohemians had left behind, a place for creating and carousing. Friedrichshagen, east of Berlin, supported one such colony.

Holz, Schlaf and the brothers Hart were joined in Durch! by Gerhart Hauptmann, John Henry Mackay, Wilhelm Bölsche and Conrad Alberti (even by the standards of 19th-century literary groupings Durch! was overwhelmingly male-dominated). But if its gender balance was stuck in the past, its mind was very much on the future, and there is an argument to be made that Naturalism was actually the first outbreak of Modernism; it certainly adopted modernity as a defining feature, as the 1886 Durch! manifesto made clear:

> Currently everything indicates that
> German literature has arrived at a turning point
> in its development which offers an outlook on a
> uniquely significant epoch.

> Our highest artistic ideal is no longer antiquity, but modernity.
>
> Modern writing should depict people with flesh and blood with all their passions in pitiless truth, without transgressing the boundaries set by the work itself, but rather increasing the aesthetic effect through the grandeur of natural truth.

Through Durch! and the later Munich-based Gesellschaft für modernes Leben (Society for Modern Life), German Naturalism rapidly became a field of intense innovation. It deployed techniques such as 'Sekundenstil' – a transliteration of the momentary in which events were recorded in 'real-time' prose analogue, anticipating 20th-century stream of consciousness. Capturing reality also meant relaying precisely how people spoke, including dialect, previously deemed unworthy of serious literature. Writers like Richard Dehmel and Anna Croissant-Rust (see *Prose Poems* in *Death*, Rixdorf Editions, 2018) were Modernists in all but name, seizing on and expanding the opportunities in form and content offered by the new style.

Unsurprisingly the provocations of the Naturalists met with censorship and outrage; Gerhart Hauptmann famously upset Kaiser Wilhelm II himself with his depiction of proletarian misery and revolt in the play *Die Weber* (The Weavers). The 'Freie Bühne' (Free Stage) provided a means to present new work on a subscription basis, thus circumventing the police permit otherwise required for staging plays in Berlin. Censors were particularly keen to keep socially inflammatory works out of the hands of the working class. Thus Émile Zola's books could be read in the original – the assumption being that their readers would be the educated bourgeoisie – but they were banned in German translation.

Once inspired by Zola, Arno Holz ultimately rejected the French writer in his quest for a total 'upheaval in art'. In 1885 he had enjoyed initial success as a published, indeed award-winning writer, receiving the prestigious Schiller Prize for his extensive verse collection *Buch der Zeit* (Book of Time), significantly subtitled *Lieder eines Modernen*. In 'Programm', an appropriately programmatic text, he announced 'No backwards looking prophet, blinded by the baffling deity, let the poet be modern, modern in his entirety!' That this battle cry was delivered in rhyming couplets undermined its point somewhat, but Holz would soon replace them with something almost unrecognisable.

Always in dire economic straits, in 1887 Holz seized the opportunity of using the unoccupied summer house of a patron in Niederschönhausen, now part of Berlin but then a town to the north-east of the city, and began working on an autobiographical novel. Recognising in Johannes Schlaf a similarly questing spirit, the following year Holz invited him to share the secluded location, which was to be their laboratory for the literature of the future, their very cohabitation an 'experiment'. Schlaf came to the partnership as a student, with a number of unpublished writings. Both were dissatisfied, their respective early careers distinguished by abandoned projects. But they sensed their time had come. In 1888, the year their collaboration began, generational change was afoot. As any German schoolchild can tell you this was the 'Three-Kaiser Year', when only the brief stewardship of Friedrich Wilhelm came between the death of Wilhelm I and the accession of Wilhelm II.

Julius Hart characterised Holz and Schlaf collectively as 'Spartans' in spirit, who 'in their art never conceded to commerce or Mammon', but he much preferred the 'soft, good-hearted, wistful, dreamy Johannes Schlaf' to the 'hard-edged, stern taskmaster Arno Holz'. Raleigh Whitinger, whose *Johannes Schlaf and German Naturalist Drama* (1997) offers the most extensive English-language account of the pair's collaboration, suggests there may have been a romantic dimension to their partnership; Holz claimed that he and Schlaf complemented each other like 'man and wife' and recalled their time together as a 'precious idyll'. Near the end of their association he provided this account which is rich in evocative bohemian detail:

> Our little 'shack' hung as airy as a bird's nest in the middle of a wondrous winter landscape; from our desks, where we sat wrapped up to our noses in large red woollen blankets, we could walk out over a snowy patch of heath which was teeming with crows, study the most wondrously coloured sunsets every evening, but the winds blew on us from all sides through the poorly grouted little windows, and despite the forty fat coal bricks that we put into the stove every

morning, our fingers were often so frozen that we were forced to temporarily stop our work for this reason alone. And sometimes we had to quit for completely different reasons. For example, when we returned from Berlin, where we always went for lunch – taking a whole hour, through ice and snow, because it was 'cheaper' there – we would crawl back into our little nest, still hungry, or when around twilight, as the colours expired outside and in the silence all around us the isolation in which we lived suddenly became audible – audible and palpable – the melancholy would overwhelm us, or when, and naturally this was always the most worrying thing, the tobacco ran out. That was heartache – impossible to describe! From Cuba we gradually sank to Caraballa, from Caraballa to Paetum optimum. Indeed once, when our need was greatest, I recall that we even smoked the last piece of an old garland. *Honi soit qui mal y pense* … Our beautiful round table with its bright velour cloth, which should actually have stood before the sofa – the 'Persian divan', as it was officially called – we had specially moved between our two desks as a worthy pedestal for the long knitting needle with which we cleaned our pipes, an empty Liebig can served as an ashtray. Finally, when the spring sky finally broke blue again through our windows, we had the satisfaction of ascertaining that our beautiful, snow-white Hermes head, which stood for so long athwart a large, red-bound Don Quixote below a little mirror, looked like a savage's skull.

The first product of this environment was the far from idyllic 'Die kleine Emmi' (Little Emmi) in which the titular young woman fends off a sexual assault by her uncle. Throughout their work, Holz and Schlaf were alert to the experience of women and the precision with which they depict Emmi's distress makes the scenario vividly real. The dialogue, too, was closer to the rhythms of authentic speech. Still, it was not quite the breakthrough Holz and Schlaf were aiming for, and for the moment remained unpublished.

For as Holz himself noted, 'You only revolutionise art by revolutionising its means.' The unlikely inspiration for the pair's definitive break with the past came with an unpublished story that Johannes Schlaf had in his portfolio when he arrived at Niederschönhausen. 'Ein Dachstubenidyll' ('A Garret Idyll', included in this collection) takes us to a top-storey household overseen by the widowed landlady, Frau Wachtel. Her tenants are an out-of-work actor and his wife plus their child who arrives and departs in the course of the story (the 'hero' of the story, as Schlaf insists), a painter who shares their bohemian disorder, and a student more aligned with the bourgeois values of Frau Wachtel.

'A Garret Idyll' is an accomplished milieu study with a pronounced sense of place inhabited by plausible figures. The frank depiction of unconventional lifestyles was unusual, but the style was still stuck in the past. Pages of establishing text – arch, prolix, syntactically sophisticated – have gone by before any of the characters speak. And when they do they express themselves in complete sentences of flawless High German, even in anger. There is irony, much of it settled on Frau Wachtel (and of course the title), but it is gentle. The presentation of the child's death is not so far removed from the Victorian cult of the dead infant but the parents' despairing response suggests they inhabit a moral universe recognisable to the average reader.

Improbably, Arno Holz saw 'A Garret Idyll' as a starting point for his 'revolutionising' of means. But his adaptation would fling readers headlong into the stream of events, leaving them little with which to orient themselves. Holz believed in the primacy of dialogue in literature, *real* dialogue, rendered with utmost fidelity to speech patterns, complete with discontinuities, inter-jections, repetitions, non-verbal utterances and a huge wealth of exclamation marks. Descriptive passages were fragmentary in exposition yet utterly precise in catalogu-ing the squalor of the characters and their environment. Once gentle, irony acquired a savage and bitter edge. You can almost *see* Arno Holz, sitting in his summer house, striking whole descriptive passages from Schlaf's story, scribbling additions. The result is 'Papa Hamlet'.

The claustrophobic setting and much of the outline of 'A Garret Idyll' survives. But the timeframe is uncertain, and there are lines of spoken text that cannot be assigned with certainty to a character or associated with a concurrent action, resulting in something more like a post-war avant-garde radio play than a 19th-century novella. The opening sentence is just one word, fittingly both question and expression of perplexity. From the scant ensuing details of the first section we are meant to surmise that Amalie has just given birth. The use of the pluperfect in the descriptive text is a further alienating factor, contrasting with the immediacy of the dialogue. The tempo of the text belies the precision with which it was produced. 'Holz often spent a whole day without getting past a sentence,' as Schlaf related of his colleague, 'because it gave him no rest, it was impossible for him to proceed before it stood before him in sparkling colours, something ringing, resounding and where possible aromatic'.

Just as striking as these features is, of course, the intertextual element – the extensive quotations from William Shakespeare's *Hamlet*, declaimed by Niels Thienwiebel and also threaded through descriptive passages. There was little precedent for a work so knowingly and rapaciously appropriating another – not refashioning or retelling, but recycling. The German translation from which 'Papa Hamlet' draws is the 'Schlegel-Tieck' version from around 1800. While certainly elevated in register, it would not have been as archaic to a German contemporary as the original would have been to a native English speaker of the same time.

It is typical of the remorseless irony of 'Papa Hamlet' that the selfish, unprincipled, deeply unreflective Thienwiebel should mouth the words of the most famously self-scrutinising figure in the Western canon, although in quieter moments he refers to himself as 'Yorick', foreshadowing his own, more ignoble death. From the liberal use of exclamation marks we can assume Thienwiebel's acting to be overwrought, contrasting with Hamlet's own advocacy of something like Naturalist performance practice ('Speak the speech, I pray you, as I pronounced it to you [...] do not saw the air too much with your hand, thus, but use all gently').

Comparing 'Papa Hamlet' and 'A Garret Idyll' reveals some astute authorial decisions. One of the most successful shifts comes in the scene where the painter's 'model' (prostitute) takes a lively interest in the young child. In 'Papa Hamlet', Holz and Schlaf (or more probably Holz, although the division of labour was a subject of constant dispute) rightly judged this brief respite to be even more poignant than the child's ultimate demise. Even across the ironic distance the writers invite us to maintain, the joy of little Fortinbras as he finally receives the simple human affection ordinarily denied him is genuinely moving.

Holz developed a reputation for formalism; Hermann Bahr, for instance, praised him as 'a strong, honest, bold talent' but 'a purely formal talent – he seeks the nature of art only in the form'. Even his own words – 'You only revolutionise art by revolutionising its means' – nudge at this conclusion. But 'Papa Hamlet' offers moments of great psychological acuity which reveal its characters' inner lives. Witness the near-catatonic Amalie Thienwiebel apathetically dunking her food in a plate overflowing with gravy, or her husband's disintegrating dressing-gown, both symbol and symptom of his physical, moral and social decay which ultimately disappears completely to leave him wrapped in a red blanket (a souvenir from Niederschönhausen).

'Papa Hamlet' presents us with a bohemian milieu, but there is little idealism, and certainly no idyll. No artistically inclined contemporary would have found in it an attractive model for living. In this dismal world we have almost no rest from the company of Niels Thienweibel, and he makes an odious protagonist, although his intensity brings anarchic energy to the claustrophobic setting. This is a work whose characters actively repel identification. They do not develop, grow or arrive at insights; instead they deteriorate, regress and accelerate toward oblivion.

It was this uncompromising desolation, as much as the experimental style and iniquitous goings-on, that proved most shocking to contemporary readers. The last section, in particular, is bracing in its abandonment of the merest human solace. Like Creation in reverse, this seventh part is sunk in darkness. Niels Thienwiebel's frosty demise following the (presumed) rape of his wife and the murder of his infant son should provide a satis-fying conclusion, but it does not. The world that Holz and Schlaf construct and populate with their little family is not equipped with a capacity for natural justice: 'Life is brutal, Amalie! Take my word for it! But – it didn't matter!' The grim ending merely suggests that the only escape from Frau Wachtel's garret is death.

'Papa Hamlet' was too short as a stand-alone publication, and Holz and Schlaf intended to issue it with two other stories: 'Ein Tod' (A Death), and 'Little Emmi'. However, the publisher – Leipzig-based Carl Reissner – felt that readers weren't ready for a tale of incestuous sexual assault and replaced the latter with 'Der erste Schultag' ('The First Day of School') for the book publication (also titled *Papa Hamlet*). This was in fact an extract from Arno Holz's unpublished autobiographical novel, in which a new pupil encounters a sadistic teacher and other childhood horrors. While there is much of interest in it, and a more expansive physical setting, it suffers from comparison with other works issued under the names Holz and Schlaf, and Holz himself later regretted its inclusion.

'A Death' (included here) returns us to the chamber setting. Like 'Papa Hamlet', it was based on a Schlaf story, this time inspired by his student days of drinking and duelling. This rendering applies an inventive Naturalist approach to a scene that might otherwise have been lifted from a Realist novel. As with 'Papa Hamlet', we are offered very little exposition, although the setting is described in fastidious detail. It is some time before we discover why we are here witnessing the passing of a young man in student lodgings. A more conventional telling might have disclosed this information then noted 'Martin babbled feverishly' and left it at that. Here, however, the delirious stream is meticulously imagined, and it is in fact the means by which we discover the duel that has brought us to this point, along with memories of first love and other fragments of Martin's brief life.

Common to 'Papa Hamlet', 'A Death' and 'The First Day of School' is a Norwegian setting imposed late in the piece to various degrees of success (least convincingly in the latter), retained even after Holz and Schlaf disclosed their authorship of the book. But the question remains – why did they (at first) assume the personae of a Norwegian writer and his translator?

In part it was a commercial consideration. Norwegians Henrik Ibsen and Bjørnstjerne Bjørnson, plus the Swede August Strindberg, were extensively translated into German and highly popular among the kind of readers Holz and Schlaf wished to reach. But there was also a sense of youthful bravado to the ruse. Witness their elaborately constructed 'Translator's Introduction' (included here) and its clichés of Nordic literature; the photo they issued of 'Holmsen' (actually Gustav Uhse, Holz's cousin); the glee with which they later exposed reviewers who had fallen for the deception – this is the drollery of the young.

It results in a dizzying construct. In *Hamlet*, Shakespeare took a character who presumably spoke Danish and had him speaking English. At some point this is translated into Norwegian for the notional purposes of this book. A Norwegian character quotes him in Norwegian and his words are 'translated' into German; to complete this conceptual Moebius strip there were even plans to have the book translated *into* Norwegian. For a work so devoid of conventional coordinates, the translation conceit served as a supra-textual distraction. Once the elaborately tooled framing device was prised away readers were faced with a work of confronting modernity.

But as we've seen, 'Papa Hamlet' *was* in fact a work of translation, with Holz (or Holz and Schlaf) rendering 'A Garret Idyll' in an entirely new idiom. Or as a Postmodern reading might have it, this was a remix. It took the original, muted some parts, turned others up until the levels were well into the red, applied echo and reverb and then dropped in samples from another work – and not just any work, but as important a text as the Western canon has to offer.

It may help to examine (the book) *Papa Hamlet* within the lineage of other pseudo-translations. The faux-foreign book seems to emerge at moments of particular instability, as if the ideas they contain are so alien to the culture into which they are introduced that they are actually badged as foreign. Much as *Papa Hamlet* launched Naturalism in Germany, pseudo-translations often stand at the outset of new traditions. Witness *Candide*, a crucial example of literary philosophy which Voltaire originally passed off as a translation from German. Or Horace Walpole's *The Castle of Otranto* – initially claimed as a translation from a much older Italian book – which launched the Gothic novel. Or reaching even further back we find *Don Quixote*, much of which Cervantes claimed to be a translation from Arabic, and which more or less invented the novel as we know it. Might it have been the presence of this volume in Niederschönhausen that gave Holz and Schlaf the idea?

In a further meta tactic, Holz and Schlaf incorporated commentary on their work into the work itself. Their next book publication, *Die Familie Selicke*, was prefixed with a Foreword that not only revealed their *Papa Hamlet* deception, but also included eight full pages of review extracts from German-speaking Europe and beyond, which remains the best source for contemporary reception of the book. And they didn't just include the raves, but the smackdowns as well, while also mischievously highlighting the critics who praised the 'translation' or the 'authenticity' of the Nordic settings.

Reviewers generally agreed that the work was savage, fragmentary and unsettling, however they were divided on whether this was a *good* thing or not. Berlin's *Die Post* may stand as representative for the latter: 'the brutality of the content is in impeccable harmony with the brutality of the depiction […] The translator is naive enough to admit in his introduction that the creations of the literary genius he discovered are "far from receiving their due in their Norwegian homeland", which fills us with respect for the literary tastes of the Norwegians …' One reviewer warmly recommended the book 'to anyone who wishes to put themselves off humanity and poetry!'; another found it to be a 'distillation of the distasteful'.

Less conservative critics reached back to the Romantics in search of a precedent, comparing 'Holmsen' with Jean Paul and E. T. A. Hoffmann. While the *Hamburger Nachrichten* found it to be a study of 'the ugly and the irrational', it felt its author 'would likely assume a leading position among his people's writers.' The *Magazine for Domestic and Foreign Literature*, the first to see through the 'translation' ruse, declared that 'Arno Holz is not only the writer who opened up new paths for Realism, he is also the only one who can proceed with complete certainty to its provisionally attainable limits in content and form.'

While the name Bjarne P. Holmsen eventually disappeared from *Papa Hamlet*, it appeared in a work that would soon eclipse it as the emblematic example of Naturalism. 'Holmsen' was the dedicatee of Gerhart Hauptmann's drama *Vor Sonnenaufgang* (Before Sunrise, 1889), even though the playwright was apparently aware that Holz and Schlaf were behind the pseudonym. The pair were initially on good terms with Hauptmann, and at one point there was talk of them writing together. But despite his dedication, Hauptmann didn't truly apprehend the implications of *Papa Hamlet*, later dismissing it as 'clumsy'. Similarly, Holz and Schlaf were initially full of praise for *Before Sunrise* – 'We believe it to be the best drama that has ever been written in the German language,' in the immoderate words of Arno Holz. But later he bitterly resented the success that Hauptmann achieved with means he held to be his own, and complained that the writer of *The Weavers* was lauded as the great 'reformer' whereas '*I* can hardly get a dog to piss on me!'

In April 1890, Schlaf and Holz published the story 'Die papierne Passion' (The Paper Passion, included here) in the journal *Freie Bühne für modernes Leben* (Free Stage for Modern Life), an offshoot of the Freie Bühne which was also closely aligned with Naturalism. Here Holz's belief in the supremacy of dialogue finds literal expression, with spoken text rendered in a larger font size, descriptive passages reduced to something like stage directions. This, and the real-time, single-setting narrative, suggests a hybrid of prose and drama.

The reference to the Sophienkirche fixes the narrative in central Berlin's Scheunenviertel (lit. 'Barn Quarter'), notorious at the time for poverty and over-crowding, with apartments, workshops and light industry sharing tenement complexes built around courtyards. The lack of living space threw together social elements that might otherwise have been kept apart and 'The Paper Passion' is an acutely observed study of the tensions that resulted. At its heart is Mother Abendroth, whose forthright profanities in Berlin dialect inevitably forfeit some of their potency in translation. She holds a degree of provisional power; her middle-class tenants will complete their studies and become better-paid professionals ('you will have long forgotten old Abendroth by then, huh?'). But even between the two students in her household there are sharp contrasts – bullish, clubbable (Röder); sensitive, awkward (Haase). The sound of the piano coming from the bel étage favoured by the better off is an audible class distinction, contrasted by the factory and its workers.

The landlady's surname, which translates as 'Sunset', invites the suspicion that it was a play on Hauptmann's *Before Sunrise*, although apparently Johannes Schlaf did actually have a landlady of that name. Her unfortunate niece Wally is another in the sorry roll call of children who suffer through Holz and Schlaf's stories. Just about everything here – the dialogue, the weather, the neighbourhood – is as raw as Old Kopelke's onions. But Kopelke himself is a pacifying influence, and his fragile creation offers a fleeting moment of grace and contemplation. The newspaper he uses for his carnival trick contains reports on the Kaiser and the criminal, the summit and nadir of society at the time, both subsumed into the Passion of the Saviour. Although Jesus is missing from this particular Crucifixion, the concurrent torment of the locksmith's battered wife, blood running down her face, suggests we should seek Christ-like suffering closer to home.

'The Paper Passion' already found Holz and Schlaf approaching the condition of theatre, and the very week it appeared their sole drama had its premiere at the Freie Bühne. Like Hauptmann's early dramas, *Die Familie Selicke* (The Selicke Family) adheres to the three Aristotelian unities (time, action, place). Drawn in large part from a Schlaf story, it synopsises the duo's thematic repertoire – alcoholism, the chamber setting, childhood suffering, young lodgers; even Old Kopelke turns up. Toying with pathos as they do elsewhere in their work, Holz and Schlaf focus on the death of the youngest member of the family – on Christmas morning no less.

*The Selicke Family* was more popular in print than it was on stage, and it is difficult to avoid the conclusion that it might have made more of an impact on audiences had Hauptmann not previously offered his *Before Sunrise*. *The Selicke Family* was the bolder work, with greater emotional force; writer Otto Erich Hartleben confessed to Holz that he had wept openly at the play. It was also praised by the esteemed Realist novelist Theodor Fontane: 'Here we are in truly new territory. Here the paths fork, here old and new part ways.'

But for now it was Holz and Schlaf who parted ways. *The Selicke Family* represented the end of their collaboration (more or less) and in 1891 they collated their works in an anthology entitled *Neue Gleise* (New Tracks), issued the following year by F. Fontane (Theodor Fontane's publisher son Friedrich). This brought together *The Selicke Family*; the three parts of *Papa Hamlet*, prefixed by a new Foreword (included here); 'The Paper Passion' and 'Little Emmi' along with two other prose pieces featuring the title character of the latter story, 'Krumme Windgasse 20' and 'Ein Abschied' (A Farewell).

The last book bearing the names of Holz and

Schlaf was one of the strangest products of the late 19th-century literary imagination: *Der geschundne Pegasus* (The Mistreated Pegasus). A large-format comic with whimsical, amateurish drawings by Schlaf and rhyming couplets by Holz, it depicts the pair themselves as imps – complete with tails – working or (more often) larking about, drinking, eating, smoking, getting into scraps. A graphic novel full of self-referential irreverence, it seems to come from a later age, but in issuing it Holz and Schlaf stood in the tradition of numerous bohemians who crafted artefacts that catered to interest in their unconventional lives among wider society. Its playfulness was difficult to square with the writers who had become brand ambassadors for urban squalor.

It certainly suggested nothing of the enmity to come. It was a dispute about their respective royalties that first drove Schlaf and Holz apart, and they now found themselves on new, diverging tracks, their experiment at an end. Many years of antipathy ensued, during which they sniped at one another from the parapets of journals, essays and books. At issue was the degree to which each had contributed to the works issued under their names; the question of *Papa Hamlet*'s origin was almost as intractable as the authorship of *Hamlet* and Shakespeare's other works.

Holz contra Schlaf played out in public, drawing numerous German literary figures into the controversy. Schlaf was wounded by the persistent suggestion that he had merely played a 'secondary' role in the partnership, or that he had supplied nothing more than the narrative skeleton which Holz fleshed out with the features that gained them such notoriety. It was a question they had, typically, addressed in their own work, initially stressing their shared contribution ('Not only do we fancy ourselves to have conducted our work in equal measure, we actually did so!').

Schlaf could rightly point to much of *The Selicke Family*, and possibly 'The Paper Passion' and other prose pieces, as his to a significant degree, even if he was applying theories that, as he acknowledged, had originated with Holz. Meanwhile Holz was eager to buttress his reputation as a great moderniser, which his work on 'Papa Hamlet' alone would appear to justify. The debate dragged on into the new century; in 1902 Holz issued *Johannes Schlaf: ein nothgedrungenes Kapitel* (Johannes Schlaf: An Unavoidable Chapter) a book-length regurgitation of the whole episode, while a 1922 dissertation by Ernst Sander made equally robust claims for Schlaf's contribution, in numbing detail.

While this quarrel left a lasting cloud of rancour over the two men's work, it also signalled the growing esteem in which these early works were held, their status as key works of Naturalism. But the movement only enjoyed a brief, non-exclusive apogee. Realism hadn't gone away – in fact Theodor Fontane was issuing some of his greatest works – and just two years after *Papa Hamlet*, Hermann Bahr was already writing of 'Overcoming Naturalism'. In 1901 Kaiser Wilhelm II gave an address in which he contrasted the artistic traditions of the past with the 'gutter art' of his day, widely assumed to include Naturalism. But by that time the movement was played out as a force in literature.

Holz and Schlaf continued to publish separately, each facing their own demons. Holz in particular emerges as a tragic figure in German letters, in no small part due to his own highly barbed nature and increasing bitterness. The great theorist of Naturalism retained his reputation as an innovator with books such as *Phantasus*, a verse collection which closed out the 19th century and offered a glimpse of the age to come. But he never knew financial security, and depended on the charity of friends. In 1929 he was nominated for the Nobel Prize (which eventually went to Thomas Mann), and he died that same year, at the time of the Wall Street Crash. His influence extended to the next generation and beyond, to the likes of Herwarth Walden, Alfred Döblin (who attended his funeral) and Arno Schmidt.

Schlaf was outwardly more successful in his later career; the year his collaboration with Holz ended he published the highly popular prose collection *In Dingsda*, and the drama *Meister Oelze*, acclaimed as a triumph of Naturalist drama. However this was followed by a number of years in psychiatric care, which ended around the time he discovered Walt Whitman, whose *Leaves of Grass* he translated into German. In the Weimar Republic he was largely active as a dramatist, while in the ensuing Nazi era he rejected the options of exile or 'inner emigration' exercised by many other writers. Instead, he – like Gerhart Hauptmann – embraced the new regime. This was not out of character; earlier works testified to Schlaf's belief in humanity as a struggle between races. In 1938, he wrote approvingly of the anti-Jewish pogroms of Kristallnacht – so much for the 'soft, good-hearted' figure admired by Julius Hart. Withdrawing from public life, Schlaf returned to his home of Querfurt, where he died in 1941.

Today, there are streets in Germany named after Johannes Schlaf and Arno Holz, while *Papa Hamlet* has even made it onto school curricula. Yet in general, Naturalism is dutifully filed away in the sequence of literary movements and rarely taken out for reappraisal, its reputation dominated by Hauptmann's earnest, heavy-handed dramas. And it is this reductive straw man that is praised or damned. Bertolt Brecht, for one, criticised Naturalism for suggesting social ills were immutable: 'To present the existing relations between people in our midst as natural, with people regarded as a part of nature, that is, unable to alter these relations, is simply criminal.' The wider significance of German Naturalism as a field of exuberant experimentation, in life as much as art, is greatly underappreciated.

The titles issued under the names of Arno Holz and Johannes Schlaf (whatever their individual contributions) offer the reduced means, moral pessimism and naked emotional force that characterise Modernism. But their appropriations, irony, self-referentiality, plasticity of form and Borgesian play of authorship make them almost Postmodern, generations ahead of time. Hopefully these compelling and inventive works, presented here in English for the first time, will find the readers they should have found well over a century ago.